ONE TRUE VOID

Dexter Petley

TWO RAVENS
P R E S S

Published by Two Ravens Press Ltd
Green Willow Croft
Rhiroy
Lochbroom
Ullapool
Ross-shire IV23 2SF

www.tworavenspress.com

The right of Dexter Petley to be identified as author of this work
has been asserted by him in accordance with the Copyright, Designs
and Patent Act, 1988. © Dexter Petley 2008.

ISBN: 978-1-906120-13-9

Designed and typeset in Sabon by Two Ravens Press.
Cover design by David Knowles and Sharon Blackie, based on a
front cover photograph by Mel Heimo.

Printed on Forest Stewardship Council-accredited paper by
Biddles Ltd., King's Lynn, Norfolk.

FSC

This book is printed on paper made
from fully managed and sustained
forest sources.

TT-COC-002303
© 1996 Forest Stewardship Council A.C.

About the Author

Dexter Petley was born in Hawkhurst, Kent and is the author of three previous novels: *Little Nineveh*, *Joyride* and *White Lies*. He translated *The Fishing Box* by Maurice Genevoix from the original French and is a regular contributor to Waterlogged magazine. He lives in a caravan in Normandy, and when not writing he is fishing or working in his organic vegetable garden.

PART ONE

one

The house was called Plato Villa. It looked shabby, even empty. Slimy old bench of rusted ironwork under a blackened willow. Rambling roses mottled and straggling. Inside was another old widow needing help shifting things about, maybe some shopping. Her name was Mrs Pollenfex. Just fetch some Chicken Supreme then tie up a bundle of newspapers and cart them down to the shed where they'll be found fifty years later.

The footscraper and bell-pull were disused, seized up, so I went down the side looking for the Tradesman's Entrance. There was a conservatory on the south side catching the sun. Inside, under the stained glare, a woman in a rocking chair. I stood watching, slowly adjusting to what I was actually seeing. She wasn't in a rocking chair. She was just rocking slowly back and forth in an armchair. I still thought I was visiting an old lady, so who was this? A nurse, because her arms were dressed in white. I thought maybe she'd put off-duty clothes on over her uniform: a pair of dungarees. But the white... Her eyes were closed, her arms were stiff... They were bandages, from her knuckles to her elbows. She must've scalded herself, and she was in pain. This was Mrs Pollenfex, then. She probably needed me to do the washing-up or peel the potatoes. I imagined her carrying a vat of boiling water, slipping on a kid's toy, her arms blistering in the spillage. I was about to tap on the glass when I saw the floor. There were dozens of pictures scattered everywhere. Coloured pastels, each portrait identical. A neck cut open, a severed heart. Christ almighty, what was going on here?

I backed away slowly till I was alongside the wall again. She couldn't see me, she hadn't seen me. Back in the porch I yanked the bell-pull, primed it a few times till it put up a decent fight. I expected to hear it bounce off the wall and crimple to the floor. I expected to wait, but she was there in seconds. I knew she must've leapt up and run. She had trouble with the door, of course. She had to walk backwards with the handle, then step aside, arms too stiff to manoeuvre. The smell was sucked out into the spring air as

3

if it had been trapped all winter. Disinfectant from the bandages, followed by a sharp stab of tobacco smoke. And then the winter apples. I fell in love with the smells first. These were the scents of the other life. Everyone has another life, all ready and waiting for them – if they can find it. Usually you wait forty-five years, and when it comes along you're too worn down to enter it. You let it float by. You spend the rest of your life with your head in your hands. But to've found it already, in Tunbridge Wells, in 1973, when I was only seventeen!

It was all there: the whole of a better life. A lament with food, a threnody with beauty. A benediction with care, an idyll with sadness. An ode with weirdness. It was a scene from my life, with Kafka and Rossetti. It was stepping through the page into an old blurred photo of the doomed. I was an exiled writer in Paris 1925. I was a poet returned from the war. I'd come to meet the decaying actress in her mansion on Sunset Boulevard. There was no room for doubt: I was that young writer come to resurrect beauty. All my precious fantasies in one.

I walked straight through a sheet of glass unharmed. It never occurred to me that she was in a parallel time. That she was trapped in a mirror. That she was really part of the doomed world I saw. And how willingly she invited me to cross over. Into that world where hands clutched straws, and lips sucked like quicksand.

– I haven't asked your name, she said.

She hadn't asked anything. I'd just walked in, closed the door behind me and followed her down the hall towards the light. Mrs Pollenfex was expecting me. I mean, it was obvious I was the student volunteer. I had my green canvas bag with a ring-file and a copy of *Middlemarch*. My hair was long and cotted. A couple of spots on my face were drying out in the spring air. My scrotty beard looked political – libertine, I should say. The hacking jacket made me look like the pencil sketch of DGR in 1848, self-portrait with black loons. The Dr Who scarf was draped at full wingspan, inches off the floor at both sides. This gave me life and movement. I was an element of the wind. My green shirt with round collars earthed me, made me pastoral enough to be visiting. The multi-coloured patchwork jumper was, of course, a hint of the neopolitan. The desert boots were just desert boots, unfortunately. But that was me all right. By chance, in all my glory.

4

There were girls at college who dressed like Mrs Pollenfex. By that I mean I didn't wonder about her age. The difference between us seemed natural and essential. She filled my world so instantly that all former values were meaningless. She appeared to me in close-up, as if I'd always seen things from a distance. There'd been no distance leading up to this. She materialized in my face. I trusted her. I'd blank myself out and say: create me. Show me.

– I'm Maxine Pollenfex, she said.

– I'm Henry, Chambers. You can call me Pisspot.

That jazz club laugh was full of smoke. She blew knowledge rings. She reeked of boredom, puked confession. She knew what it was to be ecstatic. You could see she'd negotiated her own terms with Death. I knew who she was now. My Angel of Death. She'd burned her wings off in an accident. Or the sun melted the wax. She needed me to help her fly back to the bar. Or regain the perch from which she'd fallen.

– I can't call you Pisspot, darling. I can't call you darling, either. Henry, just wait there a second.

She went into the sunlounge – glasshouse, whatever it was. I heard her trying to gather the paintings and I knew she wouldn't manage it. She came back and showed me the pastel smears all over her fresh bandages.

– The nurse only dressed them this morning. Promise me, Henry, don't look at the pictures, just help me stack them up and shove them out of sight. Promise?

– Yes. I promise.

– Under the sofa, she said. Just boot them. Well done. Can you make tea? No, let's have coffee. Do you smoke?

The kitchen was full of things I'd never eaten. Eggplant, avocados, red cabbage, olive oil, bay leaves, lemons.

I ran some water into the kettle and lit the gas. She took her coffee black with no sugar, so I said that I did too. I carried our mugs to the sunlounge and put hers on a folding table by the sofa with the ashtray, lighter and packet of Chesterfields. She offered me one and struggled to flip the top back and pinch one clear.

– I'll light it myself, I said.

– No! I have to. I want to. I'm not a fucking cripple.

– What do you want me to do? I said.

– Just keep me company, while I smoke my cigarette. Tell me

about yourself.

I wanted to melt into that sofa and keep the clock on 2.30, but I still had Miss Flack, the real old lady, to go and see. But Maxine was *so* beautiful, so powerful, that everything else could wait.

Telling Maxine about myself was all I'd ever wanted to do. I began with the essential Henry Chambers. Last week I'd been a Georgian who wrote Nature/ War Poetry. This week I was a Beat.

– I'm a Beat poet, I told her.

– Really? she said, and meant it.

– I paint too, I said.

– I don't fucking paint, she said. That's just therapy. But this is great. Listen, hey, I write poetry. I live for poetry.

I asked who her favourite poet was.

– Sylvia Plath.

– I've got a first edition of *The Colossus,* I said. Knicked it from Tonbridge Library.

I'd actually knicked it for someone else, but I could get it back.

– Knick some poems for me, Maxine said.

I promised I'd be in the glass case at Tunbridge Wells reference library that very evening. And then I did tell her everything, in one stupified sentence. Until I'd clapped eyes on Maxine rocking in the sunlounge, it was as if I'd never noticed the world around me. Like, you had to live somewhere, so I lived in Hawkhurst. Parents were just parents, old baggots moaning day in and day out, but they didn't matter. You just got on with the little discoveries you had to make yourself. But now all that was unbearable, being down in the bum class with shameful parents at a college full of Summerhill cories, dumped by your girlfriend right in front of them.

– Poor Pisspot, she said.

– How did you hurt your arms? I said.

– I hurt them, she said. Don't worry. Come into the kitchen now.

She wanted me to cut and peel some vegetables, squeeze a lemon, butter some bread, peel an orange. She said she'd damaged her tendons and couldn't grip anything properly.

– What else can I do?

– Do you really mind?

– No, but I do have to visit … this old lady …

6

– No, she said, don't go... I mean, don't go yet.

– I can come again, I said.

– Another week's no good to me, she said.

– It doesn't haff to be weekly. I can come tomorrow, I said, at two o'clock.

– Come for lunch, she said. 12.30. Will you? Promise?

– Yeah, I promise.

– Cross your heart and hope to die?

– Cross my heart and hope to die.

two

There was a life before Maxine, a defunct one I had to keep hidden, and it went like this: I was in the fifth form, Swattenden Rural Boys, just turned sixteen and the paint still wet. The School Leaving Certificates were done. I'd seen the Careers Officer in the Religious Instruction pre-fab and he said the shop floor at Diagrits was made for me. That's the plastics injection-moulding factory in Staplehurst. Moulded boys into men, but only if they fell in the machines. The mini-bus'd pick me up/take me home again, and I'd soon afford a Honda 50 after a few shifts of hard graft with all my mates. We'd chuck each other Polo Mints and sneak fags in the bogs and boast about getting a finger up last night and it'd be just like Metalwork with Fascist Fritz on Thursday afternoons. Well, I could've left school in the fourth year and got the same job, so why had I stayed in the fifth form and done the CSE? Wasn't that enough for something cushy? Just get a job and earn your keep, the Careers Officer said. The old man said this too, every time he came home in his grotty brown collar, the bully in a lawn-mower dealers' storeroom. Well, I didn't want a job, was what the old man called a 'shirker.' One of his Labour knockers. The sort of git who scrapped the TSR2.

Being working class didn't mean you had to work. There was a whole generation beginning to drift into the '70s who thought the Labour Exchange was the tool of an oppressive system. They were the middle class resistance, and my problem in life was finding a way to join them. Only it was already June, so I was leaving it late. Society had its doors open, ready to allocate me some precision tools.

At dinner break we were out in the playing fields, clinging onto childhood while the sun still shone on it, even if it was a dried-up fish with the eyes poked out. Half-borstalized boys, twenty-a-side replay of the cup final, grey jumpers for goalposts. There were four of us who wore our ties like headbands and measured the progress of our sideburns. Vowles, who actually lived near Diagrits so he could walk to work. Bill Davis, who'd just signed for Arsenal but had ginger hair growing in whiskers below his ears. And Son of Dust, the parson's boy who wore a top hat round the village and velvet loons and who'd seen Jimi Hendrix at the Isle of Wight Festival. Vowles had a tie-dye vest but wouldn't bring it to school. Bill had a skullcap he kept in his dufflebag. I didn't have anything yet, just the one sideburn I had to sellotape flat every night or it curled up – the other one so pleigic it stayed as permanent fluff round the top of my ear. So there I was, one of forty oiks kicking a Wembley-Winner round the grass, when a moped stops at the bottom of the school drive. Wow, two freaks, and they were walking into school property.

The cat had a sleeveless Afghan, red loons, Jesus beard. The chick carried a paperboy's sack and wore a purple jumper and scarlet crushed-velvet bell-bottoms. She divided a wad of leaflets between them and they began handing them out to the nearest boys, working their way across the playing fields. Price and Playfoot legged it like scared whippets towards school three hundred yards away, clutching the proof and yelping about showing sir. 'Sir' that day was Popeye, who sat in his lab lighting confiscated fags off bunsen burners. I quit the football and walked straight up to the freaks and asked for a leaflet.

– Sure, man. Here, wanna be a comrade?

They'd noticed my headband. I thought maybe the leaflets were announcing some concert in Tunbridge Wells that the old bastard would never let me go to in any case. I wasn't prepared for instantaneous conversion.

SMASH THE DICTATORSHIP OF THE HEAD!

And there was even a drawing of a pig wearing a mortar board and flailing a spiked ball and chain.

JOIN THE SCHOOLS ACTION UNION.

– Hey, I said. This is really smart. Got any more?

The chick said she was selling copies of Red Raspberry for a penny – the SAU regional mag. I paid up and rolled it into my back pocket. We were surrounded by boys now, and there were leaflets scattered everywhere, torn to shreds, balled into pellets or paper aeroplanes. I said I'd help hand them out, and I'd just got a wad in my hands when the cry went up:

– Ere comes Popeye!

It weren't just Popeye, neither. There was Raynor the dictator himself, Colonel Campbell the red bald maths fury, Games Hoppity to do the duffing, and Fritz Metalwork to swell the numbers and give it some iron. All five of them had at some point in my school career taken pure and coarse pleasure in beating, caning, humiliating or just plain thwarting me. The stand-off was comical: five masters in chalky suits, second-hand brains in a crumbling tripartite empire, at the bottom of the heap with us eleven-plus failures – and they knew it. It was not heroic; their indignation was now a fight for survival. The school was closing down and going comprehensive at the girls' school up the lane. Raynor was being demoted to deputy head.

– Get out of my school, Raynor said.

– No, you Fascist, the cat said.

– Listen to me, you long-haired yob, Colonel Campbell said. You're trespassing here, interfering with the boys. Bad show.

Hopkins started snatching leaflets off the nearest creeps.

– Give them all to me. Bring them here. At once, dammit. I saw that, Barrow. I'll strip-search the damned lot of you, if I have to.

I was standing with the comrades holding about fifty leaflets.

– Give me those, Chambers.

– Give them to me, the chick said.

I did, and Fritz made a rush at me – quite unlike him, though with the usual pith of white spittle on his lip. Pith from the gap between two front teeth like Scrabble pieces. The scientific explanation was that saliva leaked through, and the frotting of his talking lips battered the saliva whiter than white. It was Fritz and Colonel Campbell who made my fifth year totally void. Campbell did maths like army tea: boil it all up in the mess tin; sugar, milk and grouts. But, being an educated man, he sometimes declaimed Tennyson to us on wet dinnertimes. Being an oik-school, there were no Cadets for the Colonel to parade, so this was his form of patriotic brainwashing. *The Charge of the Light Brigade*, whenever it rained. So when the school governors decided that boys could have a shot at O Levels for the first time in the school's history, the

10

colonel was given English Literature. After hearing from unreliable speculators that English Lit was about reading James Bond books and seeing the films, I put my name down. I'd never read a book in my life, and even the Colonel, who had as little idea about it all as we did, made it sound like an episode from *The Man from U.N.C.L.E.* All code-breaking and plotting. No-one mentioned Tennyson or Shakespeare. We'd never heard of them. *The Charge of the Light Brigade* was, as far as we cared, written by Colonel Campbell himself. Then some late news came in from Sidney Catt's sister at Mary Sheafe's. She was doing it. One of the books was a gangster thriller and the other one was called *Animal Farm*, a cartoon story set behind the Iron Curtain.

Well, as it happened, I was the only one who put my name on the list, and Colonel Campbell said he wouldn't teach me if I was the last boy on earth. He said teaching me English Literature would be like tipping his pay down the dunny. The fact that I'd been top in English four years running only confirmed me as a cheat. My fifth year, it was decreed, would be spent in the metalwork lab where it was well known that I had no aptitude for steel and acid baths. I'd be a non-exam candidate, simply under Fritz, eye and spitz. He put me to work like a fuckin' chimney sweep too, tidying the storeroom and collecting the tin snips and iron filings. So when the little Nazi runt tried snatching my Red Raspberry I said:

– Fuck off Fritz, yer fascist.

Raynor said I had one last chance. Either throw in my lot with the SAU scum and get out of his school, or repent. Admit I'd been interfered with, and the matter would be forgotten. This is the nearest Raynor'd ever come to compassion, but it was probably politics. He couldn't afford a scandal on the eve of shutdown. He'd been appointed in my second year, thinking he was still in the Battle of Britain, diving into a nest of bandits in his Hurricane. Thought he was coming single-handed to save the great Lancaster of rural education from beasts like us who planned to take over Kent and nick all the sweets. *The Courier* made out he was a war hero. My foot, he was a war hero. I'd collected all the bubblegum cards and never saw one for Raynor, V.C. I think a brick went through his window before he'd even seen our school. He was six foot four, wore light grey suits with tiny checks, drove a shooting break bought new for the occasion. He lived in Hawkhurst too, but I never once caught sight of him. Not a village man, aloof and insensitive in a school where half the boys wore plimsolls all winter. His first contribution was to introduce rugger and hockey. It was him that recruited Hopkins to smash us on the head with a hockey stick and push our faces into a scrum for maximum discouragement. It was an easy choice for me:

– I'm with the Schools Action Union, I said, and my schooldays were over.

At the moped they called me 'comrade' and said 'welcome to the SAU.' The cat was called Laurie, the chick Briony – names I'd never come across before. New smells, new accents, real vocabulary. They said 'Power to the Pupil' with a raised fist. They said I was great and really eptitomized the struggle.

– I want to join, I said.

– That's great, man. We're from the West Kent College Branch. Yeah, we publish Red Raspberry.

– What now? I said.

– Get a place, man.

– A place?

– College, a place. It's happening...

They set off down the lane towards Benenden Girls School to give Princess Anne a leaflet. Gone like a dream, leaving me with this weird new hankering and the smell of Honda 90 smoke in an empty lane.

And in the distance, five masters herding the population of the school back into its stone age settlement, as far from me as possible.

12

three

Son of Dust lived in The Manse with his bed-ridden dad, the old Baptist Parson. His mother was agrophobic, his brother and sister were both big and lumbersome, full of combustible energy. Parkinsons had shrivelled the Parson and withered his voice. It shook and squeeked like the Sooty and Sweep Show. Son of Dust always seemed so cool, and not so much laid-back as laid-off: the subject of zero parental authority. Neither of his parents could exactly chase him outside with the dowel rod when he said he was off to some fuckin' rock festival for three days. He wasn't much to look at: fleshy and unathletic, a front tooth missing after he pulled his gloves off with his teeth and it just fell out. But he was the only genuine freak at school, which is why he didn't look like one in the playground. He called himself a 'head.' He was actually a sloth, didn't excel at anything, only at this profound calm for which he probed the source, struggling to understand human nature. Till then, he was looking for a way without Jesus interfering too much. It wasn't just the hash, which I didn't know about at school anyway. Though he was below me in the B Stream, he always seemed like a complete being. Shagging his girlfriends, piles of albums, all this amazing gear like tie-dyes, shoulder bags, top hat, crushed velvet, fringed jackets, purple vests with stars, shiny anks, leather thongs, hubbly-bubbly, hammer dulcimer. And a gang of public school freaks. They'd all applied for college: the hallowed West Kent College of Further Education in Tunbridge Wells. Freaksville, Marxtown, an underground hotbed for the far out and progressive. They were grooming themselves up for it, so I came up with Plan A: get Son of Dust to invite me in, and groom me up for college with them.

I earned a few quid strawberry picking, and bought some gear on the cheap. Aquamarine brushed cords, reduced because they were drainpipes. I made them really freaky by cutting the seams and sowing in some inserts to make loons. If they hung like two-dimensional lampshades it's because the fringes actually came off lampshades.

His mother answered the door, and said Sonny Dust was praying with his dad and I should come back another time. So I fuckin' did. People shouldn't say what they don't mean. Son of Dust was in the second time round, with a migraine. Third visit, and he came to the door, then said he was getting a job at Diagrits after all. He gave me his college application forms, but he was still adrift in the village with his cloud of freaks – or so I was told, only I never found their den. His autonomy was impressive and sage-like for a Swattenden boy. Why he wasn't at Cranbrook Grammar where he belonged, I'll never know. I kept going round there, but the freaks eluded me – hiding behind the velvet curtains, probably. At first, he was so willing and generous with the moment, too, but only certain moments: the ones he judged you mature enough to settle with and absorb without disturbance. Trying to infiltrate his inner sanctum, well, it was like I didn't have the right soul. His atmosphere was always impressionable and I tried reproducing the bits, but he could see I wasn't a suitable candidate for his perfect circle. Too jagged, too eager, not cool. In fact, I learned nothing from him about drugs or college, and he even attempted to dissuade me from both by saying he'd been thinking more about Jesus lately.

My visits obviously became more and more irksome to him. But there was something hypnotic about Son of Dust and that Manse. The way he was surrounded in the dark by all that hysterical Christian gloom. Like, I'd bang on the big heavy door with its stained glass and one by one the family would greet me like a long-lost prodigal friend, there being that line between you and Jesus. Dust's sister Delilah Dust, in her polka dot dress and a smile that went twice round her face. Even her teeth curved into a smile shape and her brace was a bullring of confidence.

– Hiiiiiiiiiiiiii, Hennnnnnnnrrrryyy, how are youuuuuuuuuuu, what have you been doing, love?

And his six-foot younger brother Seaside Dust, with the deep voice and the track and field manner:

– Hi, Hurnry. Hey, how's tricks, man? You're looking well – hey, really well.

This kid was only thirteen, for chrissake. Even his mother, Virginity Dust, said 'hi,' not *hello* or *good afternoon*.

– Hi, Hen love, she said, God be with you, sweetheart.

And sometimes the old Parson, Doom and Dust himself, was peeled from an armchair commode in his study upstairs, wobbly cane banging out a Ginger Baker drum solo.

– Here's Henry, Parson Dust. Come to see Sonny. Do you want to say hi?

And as if it was the condition of a sadistic nurse, he stammered and stuttered in his tea-stained suit till up it came:

– Hhhhhhhhhhhhhhhh-hi HHHHHHHHHHHHH-Henry.

No-one else in the village said *hi*, only Baptists. I thought maybe it was some kind of universal familyhood, natural happiness, but it wasn't. They were all under the throng of Parson Potter and his wife Parsnip, young committed bigots who'd been to America and seen the Baptist revival and a few alien takeover B-movies. Our village was his first flock. A year back, he moved into a bare bungalow beside the chapel while they revived the big Manse out near the Dusts. At first, his congregation was a hand-me-down row of the mentally ill. So he launched The Crusade, The Covenantors, and The Baptist Youth Fellowship. For him, Bible Belt meant below the belt, and he concentrated on the three stalwart Baptist families of the district, working outwards through networks of sons and daughters. The campaign was actually driven by the organist, a self-made man and pioneer of pyramid selling. So, instead of household cleaning fluids we got soul cleansers, pyramid Jesuses scouring out the Devil from the germs round the toilet bowl of rural youth. This way, he struck a rich seam of public school freaks with shitty arses, and he went for them. Cats and chicks, as if he ran a stray dog pound, filled the fuckin' church with barking nutters who could've been my friends.

Obviously, I'd misunderstood. Son of Dust's wisdom was weariness all along. My applications to get together with him and his Heads were always politely rebuffed or cleverly side-stepped. I knew they took long walks round the village or sat strummming guitars in joss-stick-reeking dens someplace. It was only a matter of being in the right place at the right time. The more I craved this intimacy, the more of a prat I felt, so the more I needed them to deliver me from this condition.

One afternoon, acting on a tip-off, I bumped into them, the whole inner circle taking their Sunday stroll. Son of Dust with his hollow black-eyed Judy Biba spacewalked out of Jefferson Starship.

Brim Stone with his guitar and beard walking along strumming *Streets of London*. His pregnant chick Flick with her cadence of blonde hair and silver shades. Brim's brother Treacle, the public school tart, with his beautiful lips and pudding-basin haircut, newly expelled for immoral activities. His chick René, another pupating one in purple, six months up the weasel. So both Stone boys had their chicks bunged up, and I could see Son of Dust wished he'd never told me that. It'd been a confidence divulged as a reason why I shouldn't be there when any of them called round The Manse, owing to all the heavy vibes, owing to the fact that none of the parents had noticed and all meetings were fraught discussions on how to maintain the subterfuge into the ninth month. Flick wore cunning bun-disguising capes and only went home when it was dark. René was a whisp with hardly a bump under the flowing gowns. Only problem was, the Stone brothers' old man, Tomb Stone of Jesus himself, was the Pyramid Pope, the Baptist church organist and the Parson's nose.

The way they reacted when they saw me, christ, you'd think I was the answer to their prayers. All that *great to see you, man* stuff, the linked arms and the *walk with us, Henry, really far out man, really groovy, hey*. Well, I was scared and excited. We were even heading for Little Switzerland where I knew I'd be offered the peace pipe, my first ever taste of resin.

– Hey man, how's it going? What's new?

– Oh, you know. I've been writin', axshully.

Huh, my first story, a moving dirge called *My Last Day at School*, for Red Raspberry.

– Hey, Henry, that's far out. Jesus loves you, man, Brim Stone said.

I thought he was joking, but then Son of Dust said:

– That's right, that's really truly right. The Lord's proud of you, Henry.

After only three hundred yards, Dust said:

– You'll have to excuse us now, Hen. I'm not being rude, man, but we've some really heavy vibes to sort out, yeah?

– Yeah, Henry, truly truly sorry, Brim Stone said. But hey, I'd really like to find out what you're writing, man. Hey, great idea: why not meet us all down the church at half-six?

– Yeah, that's groovy, Dust said.

16

– That'll be far out, Flick said.

– You think so, Judy Biba said, which gave the others face-ache.

– It's cool, Dust said. Don't sweat, babe. You know, Hen, we just hang around and play games, sing songs, yeah? Nice people, really nice groovy people. Plenty of sounds, Mum does the refreshments, you know? The Parson drives her down, it's the only place she goes now, Henry. You know how it is, you're like, part of the family…

I fell for it. I was there, for fuck's sake, 6.30 sharp. Even more lonely than thick. Sixteen, but old enough to be fucked by God, old enough to marry Jesus with parental consent. Parson Potter, Parsnip and the Parson's nose were all there to greet us. I was introduced, my hand was shaken, held, patted, warmed.

– Hi, Henry, it's great to see you here. The Lord welcomes you. The Lord is proud of you. Jesus is waiting for you inside, so come on in and meet him.

They'd planned it, the Judas creeps. They'd made a pact with Jesus to get away without retribution for shagging their chicks by bringing in the lambs. Parson Potter gave his supernatural sermon, the Bounty of Jesus. *Friends, the Lord provideth, believe me. I was driving home last week when I ran out of petrol…* He'd stood in the road and prayed to the Lord: fill my tank, Lord. When he walks round to the boot there's a full can of petrol sitting there. Yeah, fill it yer fuckin' self, Parson, the Lord must've said.

But they believed him. They all believed him. They clapped and shouted praise for the miraculous benzine. My instinct, no doubt base and Swattenden, was to stand up and shout 'you lying cunt, Potter." I looked at my fellow freaks for support, beside me in the third row of these over-polished pine coffin-wood pews. Dust and Brim Stone were nodding. Flick was swinging her feet. Treacle Tart was grinning, I hoped contemptuously. His chick was either bored rigid or ashamed of herself. They knew what was coming: the Parson opened his arms wide and said it was time for the Lord to reveal himself. Great, the free mug with every gallon. Stand up and bear your witness, turn out your pockets for Jesus…

Son of Dust and Brim Stone were on their feet like Jack-in-the Boxes. Flick was fighting Jesus for an instant, but Brim Stone held out his hand and she rose in hypnotic defeat. A look of pain passed between the two brothers, not least because their father was playing

17

a Stones riff on the organ like the big moment on *Take Your Pick* when Michael Miles says 'Take your pick, open the box.' But they all rose, they knew they had to, their sins were huge dirty stains to know-all toe-sucking Jesus.

Dust kicked off in the witness stand.

– I want Jesus, like, I really want the Lord to come in my heart. I've sinned against Jesus. I've sinned against my parents, against the church, like, I'm ashamed, man. I've taken drugs, yeah, and I've committed lewdness with my woman...

But his woman wasn't there, neither. Judy Biba had fled to Tunbridge Wells. She could've warned me. Then Brim Stone almost shoved Dust aside to get his own witness in. This was gang rapture. He'd committed the same sins against the same people, smoked the same shit, done the same lewdness, but, but... And his old man was whiffling away on the organ soundtrack, his blue nylon tie swishing like a cow's tail chasing flies, his pink shirt rolled up at the sleeves. When we reached that 'Open the box' moment, Brim Stone said:

– Flick is with child. Oh, Jesus, save her, help her, Jesus.

The organ pooped itself into *Ivor the Engine*. Poooop-poop and there were cries from all round the pews:

– Oh, my son. Get on your knees and pray...

One of the mentally ill shouted: Stone the harlot!

Brim Stone was on Gethsemane-black – had to be. God-arsed, fuckingpebble-dashed his brains, confessing to every crime since World War I. Flick was clapping, perhaps to drown his voice out. She looked belly-up now, even if she didn't before. She was probably hoping her mum wouldn't hear through the walls, because she only lived next door. Me, I was edging my way along the pew when Brim Stone opened his arms, on his way to Heaven with the siren going.

– Treacle, my brother, come with us. Henry, my friend, come with us, man. You're not free of sin, and it's great out here with Jesus, you guys.

It was like a prank gone awry. Jesus still hadn't come through that vestry door. And what were my sins? I hadn't done any yet. They hadn't let me, the toe-rags. Treacle was still clinging to the pew with me, and René was clinging to him. We were all clinging to the space where Judy Biba should've been. Brim Stone wasn't moving us, so he resorted to Parson's tactics.

18

– Pray, you good people, for my brother. Jesus, saviour, implore him to step into your Father's arms to cleanse the sin in René's belly.

– Wow, you bastard, Brim, Treacle said.

– You poof, Treacle. You sodomite! Brim shouted back.

Treacle and René were on their feet and pushing out. Son of Dust led the congregation in their shouts of *shame, harlot, vileness.* The Parson's nose was off his organ and shouting for his sons to get on their knees and pray as they'd brought shame on the family Stone. Parson Potter was preparing this awful Baptismal pit set in the floor out front and full of the river Jordan, specially diverted from Palestine to come out the vestry tap. His face was that of a man about to drown the puppies, not baptise the converted. Sink like a Stone, we would've.

Then Flick broke free and ran for the door. Within twenty seconds she'd be locked in her bedroom and I'd be the only one left. I'd missed my chance a second time, frozen to the pew, hiding under the flack of all this Sodom and Gomorrah going off around me. They'd run out of sinners, and Dust held his arms out as if he'd been given the church as a big Wendy House to play Parson in:

– Hen, Hen. You can do it, man. Join us, join Jesus. Find your friend in Jesus. Forget those ideas about experimenting with drugs and Communism. Write for the Lord. God is for real, man, get high on Jesus…

– Jesus makes me sick, I said, thinking more about the laurel leaves and cinnamon I'd had to smoke instead of the real thing. Thinking: damn, weeks of bum-sucking wasted. I'd have to score a quid deal on Hastings seafront now.

I was at the door this time as if I'd sat on the Burning Bush itself. Parson Potter soon changed his tune from the welcome mat. He'd slipped into his Klu-Klux Klan robes to get into that pit with sinners. The whole fucking church echoed behind him.

– You've got the devawl in yer, Hen. The Devawl! The Devawl! Let me cast him out!

four

Thursday afternoons in Liberal Studies, you got the afternoon off college to follow an activity. Sport or social service. The Christian rambler who co-ordinated the voluntary work was a spotty straight called Keiran. Orange windcheater, hiking boots, he organised the Geography field trips and other zeal-related events. He said I was the only student signed up for the domiciliary. He gave me the old toad's name and address: Miss Flack, Camden Chase House.

First sight of the house was spellbinding. It occupied an entire island in the centre of a cobbled square off Mt Sion. I was sucking my teeth just at the size of it: six three-bed council houses easy, and all the lights were on by the look of it. Bounded by high walls it was, a long house of seventeenth-century brick and weatherboard. I thought: bunk-up, some patronage. I unlatched the gate, almost kicked it open. I was in my Pre-Raphaelite kit too, lady's horsehair hacking jacket, black loons washed drab, desert boots dying of thirst, ten yards of scarf trailing in the grit, my college folders in the green canvas fishing haversack I'd had since I was thirteen.

I walked up the long brick path between rose bushes, bird tables, white wooden benches, a limp willow, tangled crab apples and a sun-dial. The first rags of snow fell, and it was like coming home after a bracing stroll.

As I stood at the outer door and looked for a bell-pull, something caught my eye. Pinned to the inner door. Fire Regulations. Assembly point 1. Then something caught my nose. Residential cooking, stinking up the hallway, coagulated gravy, meatbally, mashed potatoey. The walking stick stand was full of walking sticks and vice-like callipers. By the table with the letter racks and potted plants was an old trout in horn-rims, shingled grey hair and a back so arched that only a stout cane stopped her toppling forward. She peered at me rudely like a toad, eyes rolling forward as I ran my finger over the house plan on the wall. Miss G.Flack, 2nd floor, room 19.

I followed an arrow to the foot of the stairs. Beside Miss Toad sat a man with ears like tree-fungus, dentures clacking every wheeze. Miss Toad shrilled at him:

– That'll be the doctor now, Mr Whitewick! Or some nurse I've never seen before.

– Rubbish, Miss Boxall, the dentures said. It's only Miss Flack's niece in her hunting outfit.

It was all shame and disappointment – the sort you can't swallow, which clots in your throat like a raw egg. The footman, the conservatory tea, the grand portraits and dusty volumes I'd conjured up seconds before all turned to geriatrix. I was in an old peoples' shelter. Well, a home for the active elderly. The kitchen was staffed. I could smell the truth, I could hear all the ex-school dinner ladies banging aluminium cauldrons the other side of rubber swing doors. I could see the active Miss Boxall swivel on her stick and fix her death wish on me.

Gilt-framed mirrors, bookcases on every landing with dead flies and whodunnits and book club editions in faded covers. Agatha Christie, Dorothy L Sayers, Margery Allingham… Small tables with rickets, shells arranged in symmetrical patterns on tea-trays. The bogs had red lights over the doors and painted wooden discs dangling on a piece of string. Green for GO, red for DON'T. Every room had a number and a name-slip in a brass holder screwed to the door. In one far corner of the top landing where the roof angled down, there was a wide latched door and a name slip which said:

Miss Gregoria FLACK.

I knocked.
– Come in!

A high, soft-pitched but commanding voice in drag, or was it being ironic, poised to drop like an anvil? She said, later on, that when I walked in she knew there was a green crow in the air. I forget exactly what a green crow connotates – my great word of the day – but it was something to do with Louis MacNiece and Ireland and chains of favourable, connected events.

She was right, because you didn't forget a moment like that in a hurry. First the brass-railed bed rumpled like the Welsh hills, the storm sky of a ceiling coming down right on them. A moulded dip in the middle with a bolster marked the place where Miss Flack sat or lived or something – I just couldn't imagine what. The rest of the bed was cluttered with books and papers which overflowed onto a table and off a stack of luggage trunks. Everything was bound in string and elastic bands or yellowed sellotape. Poetry anthologies, twenty-year-old copies of *The Listener, Radio Times, Poetry Ireland*; tattered volumes of Robert Graves, Keith Douglas, David Jones. A wooden Roberts radio strapped up with an old belt.

Then I was inside, bashing my brains out on the beams. I saw behind the door, the opposite corner under the gabled window. The flip-side. Turned me cold, it did. A white enamel bowl with something grey soaking in soda, a bucket of discarded bandages, boxes of medical tissues, soiled gauzes, a smell of ointments.

Miss Flack was standing by the wash basin emptying steam from a Brown Betty teapot. A heavy, solid, short woman in a thick tweed skirt, a hump of cardigans, legs like bandaged pillars which it'd take Samson to topple over.

– Hello, chum, she said. Come on in properly and sit you down.

The room was so cramped and cumbered and Miss Flack's hooded eyes so slow and sure in seeking me out that we just circled on the spot and got tangled in scarves and string. There was only this winged sofa-ette with horsehair sticking out to sit on.

– Coats away, Miss Flack said. Books and papers where you will.

I stacked up seven biscuit tins full of papers then sat with a few pet Fabers on my lap. The cosy sat nicely on the teapot and a tiny round table was wheeled over, lumbered with Dundee cake, almond slices, butterfly-shaped sandwiches and cheese straws. What was going on? Who was this Miss Flack, with her sepia verse and the tweed undertones?

My encounters with grannies up to then were all bad. Life-long feuds with half of Kilner Road. In the end, they all merged into one dried-out old gusset, all the Hector Haunts, the ga-ga Mr Follingtons, old Ma Aids, Miss Burns, Nina Langleys. Hector Haunt tried a truce once, the silly old dod. Told me all about life as a boy before World War I, working on the trams in Sheffield when he was fourteen. He'd got a white beard and drove a blue three-wheeler. When our ball went over he chased you to the gate, the fuckin' beetroot. But

Ma Aids was worse. The ball either went over Hector Haunt's fence or Ma Aids' hedge. She taught me all I needed to know about the succession of age. I was born where she lived. She took over no. 9 that same winter when they moved us down to the corner. A gizzened-up widow, bereft of all indulgence for kids. She struck like a pike to confiscate stray footballs before you'd even climbed the gate. She was one of those mythical pike created by a German bomb falling on the village pond, a mouthful of rusty grappling hooks and trails of snapped line from her contests down the years. The old bats in their belfries were our entertainment when I was at school. She thrilled us to the screech, trussed like a dried ham in stiff black skirts and shin-pad blouses. Ma Aids creaked in the heat, head-scarf knotted under her chin, walking stick you'd beat the donkey with. She could crack a walnut in her gums, she tied her discarded bloomers round her plants, and still slopped out with the clanky old bucket we left behind by accident all those years back. We had to shin over her gate because her son Eamon, who came Wednesdays in his brogues and tweed and beetroot shaves, rolled a length of telegraph pole up against it, chainsawed it himself. Then he publicly executed our footballs with Aida's carving knife and our folk did nothing, didn't even stand by and laugh. That's what I thought Miss Flack'd be like: not a poet who drank tea with WB Yeats in 1933; not Maxine Pollenfex's giddy aunt.

five

The day I met Maxine, they still called me Pisspot. Slags did, scrubbers, all them prongos whizzing round the village on their Motobecanes. I knew who they meant. He was made of all my spare parts and could easily have tipped the balance in his own favour. To them, I was possessed by someone else. Parson Potter's devil, the weirdo Pisspot to all the kids I used to play with. They didn't understand why I wasn't hanging about up the chip shop with them any more, or phlobbing cheese and onion curd outside the public bar up The Oak, or playing inside left for the second team. Pisspot, they shouted. Yer muvver's! So did the baggots, in their own language of course: Henry, yer bloomin' knocker!

I was motivated for greatness, but the trouble was the only motivation known in the working class was the thing your old man struggled with under the bonnet of a Sunday morning. Any struggle just wasn't going to survive that kind of dialectic.

I didn't know you had to have a vision of yourself till Miss Flack put me straight. If I wanted to be a poet, she said, I had to have a vision of myself. That was the radical step for me. I was too busy catching up on just the words. There was no room for mission, no time for traction. This girl at college had already written a hundred pages of a novel. She'd said to me: well, what are you going to be? I had no vision whatsoever, and she sat somewhere else. That was family heritage, that was the working class syndrome – something my collegiates couldn't grasp. The pointlessness of trying, the failure on the doorstep, the cruel magnitude of example. The way you had to lie your way out of a mess if you weren't born with the fruits of existence dripping off your trees. I didn't have the glamour. The co-eds, the Jollyons, the Crispins, driving to college in their purple Beetles and yellow Minis, money for Nukey Browns and ploughmans down the Sussex. The Lucindas and Virginias eating their cottage cheese in the music room on their viola cases... I epitomized the class difference, not the struggle. They couldn't even say the words 'working class.' They called us the 'proleteriat,' as if we were graced with political recognition.

I just looked the brick wall in the face then, and continued sending my First World War poems to *Outposts*, throwing away the kind rejection slips that old dog's beard Mr Sargeant wrote by hand. Bury the talents and the rage impotently, within the working class tradition of pessimism. The old man was still running the family like Dad's Army, too, in a house full of Iron Curtains, Berlin Walls, a Cold War in every unheated room. Real life became like stuff you got told at school, facts you didn't care about. People were obstacles you learned to avoid. Everything I wanted was on a short string, caged and tethered. The more I read, the more I felt cheated.

Like, for years, the old man made me line up on my own, standing to attention every Saturday morning for my pocket money which I was obliged to put into the black piggy-bank under the stairs with its sprung slot and satisfying clunk. And one day it would be full and I'd be able to buy my freedom. The fuckin' gas meter wasn't it.

The Jollyons had no gripes about their own folks, as they called them, except that they saw life as a game of chess. One Jollyon said it was 'a walk across a ploughed field in the pouring rain.' Oh, please. Well, my baggots thought life was a game of draughts in the filthy drizzle. Black and white, poor man's lot, stay on the square and narrow or get jumped on. It was as if we'd never noticed each other before I hit college. The boy was job-fodder. Sixteen and pay your keep, shut your brains up like an old schoolbook and welcome to the university of life. The baggots had bleakness down to a fine art, the working class ethic kept in a teapot on the mantlepiece. Every day was a rainy day. The fruits of life were regulated. A bottle of Mackeson and a Mars Bar on Saturday night with ITV. One week's holiday a year when you wash the car, mow the lawn and paint the kitchen yellow. The old bag's idea of bliss was doing the ironing on a Sunday night listening to *Sing Something Simple*. I was supposed to inherit and cherish this vision of life as if it was a bag of knitting patterns from out of the bottom drawer.

It wasn't their fault, I suppose. The boy was suddenly a weirdo with subversive ideas that only a clip round the ear would see off. I was an Enemy in the house. Sociology, poetry. Choosing my own clothes. These were like Russian nuclear weapons to the old bastard. Nothing like *that* saw off the Germans. At my age, the old woman had stood at her front gate in Gravesend clapping the Aces in their

Spitfires as they dogged off Jerry 109s over Kitchener Avenue. At seventeen, the old man was able seaman Chambers, plying the Atlantic, painting bollards and peeling the steel grey waves for U-Boats. And would they let me forget it.

– You step out of line once more, my lad, and you'll be packed off to Diagrits on the next bus. Biggest mistake we ever made, letting you go t' bloomin college.

They'd invited me to an interview for the A levels, me and a parent. The old man grudged himself an afternoon off work and moaned about making up the lost wages. Just so I could carry on spongeing. We sat side by side before the principal's desk, pinching up our trouser knees like serious men. The principal was bored rigid, so he asked the old bastard what he thought about it all.

– Not much cop, if you ask me, poetry. In the work-a-day world.

The principal wondered if I had any response to that. I told the paperweight, a lion from Trafalgar Square, that I didn't know. The old man unlaced a shoe during a yawn which went round all three of us. He said I only wanted to go because I was a shirker. Then he rolled the sock off his foot under the desk thinking we couldn't see and fungled the toe-nail clippers from his key-ring. Two blackened frags tiddlywinked into the wastebin.

– Given your objection, Mr Chambers, what would you hope your son might gain from an education? the principal said.

– I think it's plain daft. Jackin' in the chance of a good job just to read bloomin' po-tree. If y'ask me, the boy weren't born with enough gumption that a few years workin' won't put back. Books never interested 'im before an' no good'll ever come of it.

He heard them calling me Pisspot, too. Polishing the car, he was, as I was setting off with my pen and inks for Little Switzerland, off on what the old bag called one of my 'painting jaunts.'

– Pisspot, yer muvver's.

It was only fuckin' Snoggit with nothing to do, but instead of rounding on the squirt, the old man chucks his googly at me :

– Look what's become of yer, boy. The way you are, even the whippersnappers don't respect yer. Thinking y've bettered yerself with yer airy-fairy bloomin' ideas and dressin' like an I-doan-know-what – a scarecrow. God almighty, earn some respect.

– Where's respect ever got you? I said.

– By Gawd, Henry, you're not too old for a belt across the jacksy...

I'll tell you where respect ever got him. A late mid-winter afternoon in 1962 it was, the day our family motto was born. *Crying Shame.* I don't know what that is in Latin; it was never translated. We went in the Austin A30 to visit this posh widow near Rye. I was seven, this was my first lesson in respect for the betters. The old bag had emptied all her Christmas Yardley over her best dirndl. I'd been skin-grafted white and forced into hand-knits. The old man had picked the moth-balls off his demob suit and brushed his trilby. Posh widow lived in a converted Post Office overlooking the river Cuckmere. She had such airs and graces, she made us wait in the car while the old man was in the house with his toolbag. At teatime she handed us rattling second-best china cups through the car window, then went all tessy, shouting because her daughter Judith had eloped with Vincent, the builder who'd come to fix the boiler. He'd slipped rendezvous notes under the toilet soap and they'd courted in secret down in the churchyard. Posh widow said right in front of us that Vincent was just a common handyman, had long sideboards, wore a white rollneck and winklepickers and drove a wretched Mini-van. This was curtains in our house too, and I tutted along with the others. Posh widow blamed the telly, saying this Vincent looked like some bloody criminal in *The Saint.* Well, I'd said 'bloody' once and the old man'd all but wrenched off a table leg to beat me with, saying if I ever swore again he'd tan my living hide. But not Posh widow. They were hanging on her every word, nodding and tutting and saying 'dear me.'

On the way home you should have heard them licking her boots. What a spicey character, that Ma Twallin. What class.

– Yerse, the old bag said. Weren' right what that ... what he did...

– Awkward, havin' fella like that comin' rarnd. Nice Jane like Judy too. Cryin' shame, if truth be told. Cryin' shame...

Thus was born the family motto. Any slight to our betters, any bother to interupt the felicity of the middle classes, was a cryin' shame to be put right by good old Mac and his toolbag. And I'd better not forget who I was.

– Pisspot, yer muvver's!

So who was this Pisspot, then, about to defy the toolbag on

his way to Maxine Pollenfex? If I took Pisspot's weekend walks, I also shared his early life. I suppose the way to describe him is as if he was supposed to be my small shadow in a high sun, my future in an altered state. My projected failure, my vomit. I still slept in his bed. He was me squared, plus the cubic root of pi, that part of me that girls noticed. A girl's point of view, which in a village with only comparison, no similarities I knew of, meant derision and amusement. Pisspot was the receptacle of my disappointment, my father's son, my mum's boy, the carcass for the body of their ignorance, the counterweight on my mind, this brother-brawn. He was my future if I didn't pull something off, if something didn't happen and I didn't get that vision of myself and become a poet or a working class hero in the middle class itself.

When you're sixteen/seventeen, you don't know what it is. You don't know what anything is. At first you can't even name it – you don't know if it's friend or foe, but you know it's there and to do with Hawkhurst, where you live, the only place you've ever lived. This invisible swarm, when you're flapping at nothing, or you're exausted by too much energy. You reach for poetry but that's just sprinkling iron filings on your own magnetic field. You analyse yourself but that's just brass-rubbing your own personality. You don't see it or nothing, you're in a state of double negatives. You've got lead flashing on your collars, a lost voice, contracting walls. Every Sunday's a Wednesday afternoon. It's walk walk walk walk. Closed shops, closed signs hanging on your future. It's a joke: hey hey, everyone's a posh widow … but there's no punchline. Just a punch. You keep going up the cemetery yourself on the off-chance that all the Pre-Raphaelites buried there might've come to life. You can hear things you never heard before, like the silence of mud-filled sucking hollows. Or the sunlight cupped over deadened council estates. And talk about second sight! You can see the previously invisible: the merciless unquenchable emptiness of the rest of your life. And that echo in the distance about to cross the horizon, it's what you could've become, leaving you behind.

Your walk walk walk walks start with skiving college and become compulsive journeys after signs. It's as if you've found a parallel world along the Hawkhurst lanes and footpaths. The footprints, dog-ends, used jonnies, miles of snagged 8-track, boxes of switch gear dumped by pissed-off thieves, porno mags stashed by lorry drivers. There're people in these shadows. In your crying shame you're after anyone, but you start at the top of the list. None of the girls at college want to slum it with you. The Claires and Virginias of West Kent College have James and Jollyon as their social equals. Not Henry the quiet smelly poet with the tumbleweed bumfluff beard and cotted hair, the only student in college whose parents wouldn't let him go on the camping weekend at the start of term, where everyone sat round camp fires listening to The Yes Album and baking potatoes and making friends for life. The old bastard had said: no, you bloomin' well can't go dossing in the woods with a bunch of beatniks. You can stay in sight where we know what you're up to. So there is no-one for you: no Pre-Raphaelite stunner, no stunner look-alike, no goofy art student in Kensington Market togs no-one else'll talk to. The list is long but you go down it like a greased pole. At the bottom it says: try for a mere aquaintance.

So you choose an ex co-ed who sat next to you in Chaucer once, at the beginning of the first year, when he showed you one of his poems. Crispin Ogilvy. He drives the purple VW Beetle into college. His old man keeps wallabies in his Sevenoaks conservatory. But after the camping do, he's found all his kindred equals and sits elsewhere. You go up the phonebox ten times before plucking up the guts to dial it. You're gonna ask him if he wants to start an art movement, then come out to Hawkhurst and pick you up in his Beetle. He'll introduce you to his pater and you'll see the wallabies. But his mater answers and says what you already knew. Crispin's at Belinda's for the weekend.

There's no-one. So you want foster-parents, step-parents, jailers. HELP POLICE ARREST ME! I'M MUGGING MYSELF. Fuck me, a talking horse would do. You invent a ghost, one of Christina Rossetti's rejected suitors because you … are … just … so LONELY. The thing is: you were born a snig, they weren't. You're at the bottom of the list now, and it says ME. ME has no sophistication, for a start, something Crispin and Jollyon must've noticed. So you write yourself that first letter, an invitation to a little cultural get-together with yourself if you can't have your little tea with WB Yeats. You know sweet fanny adam about wine – you've never tasted wine. You've saved up your pocket money and you buy this yellow-looking wine from the new off-license in the village, the cheapest bottle on the shelf. You sit at the sheep's-fat yellow kitchen table while your baggots watch *Kojak* in the front room. You can hear the old man cracking toffee with a toffee hammer and calling everyone on telly a loud-mouthed yank. But you're at a soirée like the ones Miss Flack described to you. The condensation runs down the freezing window and the sill smells of trapped rot. It's the Latin Quarter, it's Trastevere, SoHo, Greenwich Village, and you're a Libertine, a working-class hero, a Bohemian, and you're talking to them! Your stunners, your wallabies, your horses, your ghosts. Cheeselet stunner? Cream cheese with sort of 'erbs, 'orse? Yah yah yah; oh, you like Satie, then, Wallaby? Trouble is, that fuckin' horse prefers Led Zeppelin. You think the railways are more important than religion for the future of social cohesion in Europe, eh, Stunner? The kitchen door flies open, your old man says 'turn that blessid racket down.' No more invitations from yourself arrive. You're not even on your own Christmas card list.

And then, just as you're putting the black edges round your own stationery or plotting to murder your baggots, a beautiful woman old enough to be your mum takes you in her bandaged arms and makes you promise to die for her.

six

I was sent to Maxine due to a small chain of events which began innocently enough. Miss Flack was always looking for ways to boost my esteem. Since she'd been so very pleased with my 'helping hand' visits that winter, she decided they should be recognised. She typed a note to the college, thanking them and praising my kindness. Typed it, because years of speedwriting had left her calligraphy looking like scribble. She was wondering, she typed, if some similar kindred spirit might not be sent to her niece, who also found herself in temporary distress. Of course, she had a girl in mind, not me.

Kieran, the grim Christian, told me about Miss Flack's note because no-one else was doing these domiciliary visits, and Social Services had already asked him to send someone to this same house in Calverly Park mentioned by Miss Flack in the letter. A woman needed help shifting things about, maybe some shopping. Her name was Mrs Pollenfex.

It was revision term by then; the first A Level was a month away. The air was suddenly as warm as Sunday bed. The smell of lilac, the lime trees scolding green, the fields had that whiff of plasticene and tobacco jars. I'd heard a cuckoo over Little Switzerland. I'd seen the swallows hurtling round the village barns, trout rising down Ockley Pool. I'd made a working pact with loneliness. I thought I knew what my life would do from then till October, as sure as any seventeen-year-old who'd accepted a place at Swansea. A Levels would be a walkover: two Bs and I was in. The old man's belly-aching had become like road drills two streets away. You just got used to it and took the long way round. I only had to endure myself till June. Then, it would all change. I'd be on my way and he couldn't stop me. The Hawkhurst void would fall on someone else.

In the meantime, I was content enough to go knock on another old widow's door and fetch her that Chicken Supreme and a packet of moth-balls. The house was called Plato Villa, and the irony didn't strike me at the time. It looked empty, even shabby. Slimey old bench of rusted ironwork under a blackened willow. Rambling roses mottled and straggling.

The red brick path was moss-green and flecked in white scab of sparrow shit. The rotten bird table, once painted brown. The window frames needed a lick of paint and the porch was packed in dead leaves blown up against the door. A pint of milk with the cap pecked through. There were woodlice where I kicked the coconut mat. The footscraper and bell-pull were disused, seized up, so I went down the side looking for the Tradesman's Entrance.

It was a 'between seasons' garden. A poet's garden, where time had extra stanzas. It had those inter-regnums that other gardens didn't share. The sad periods were extended, like nature's gothic, as if poems were just shade-loving plants. Those corners you can only see with the corner of an eye. You didn't need blue plaques on the wall when you had the actual poem still living there.

There was a conservatory on the south side, catching the sun. Inside, under the stained glare, a woman in a rocking chair. I stood watching, adjusting to what I was actually seeing. It wasn't a rocking chair. She was just rocking slowly back and forth in an armchair. Who was she, then? A nurse, because her arms were dressed in white. I thought maybe she'd put off-duty clothes on over her uniform: a pair of dungarees. But the white ... her arms were stiff, her eyes were closed. They were bandages. She must've scalded herself, and she was in pain.

This was Mrs Pollenfex, then. She probably needed me to do the washing-up or peel the potatoes. I imagined her carrying a vat of boiling water, slipping on a kid's toy, her arms blistering in the spillage. Or was it a re-occuring, life-long debility, reflected in the neglect around her? I felt compelled to hurry and relieve her anxiety at being helpless and hurting. I was about to tap on the glass when I saw the floor. Dozens of pictures thrown everywhere. Curled, crumpled, flat, draped, torn, all on sugar paper three feet by two. Coloured pastel portraits, each identical. An olive brown woman's head or face. A bald head with huge eyes. A broken nose, full lips. Tears ran from one eye. There were thorns on the scalp, droplets of blood. In some, a wedding veil in flames. Wedding flowers stripped of half their petals. There were some other variations: the ones nearest her too, the ones in her head, now. A neck cut open, a severed heart. I'd seen pictures like these at college in Theory of

Art. A South American painter called Frida Khalo. Christ almighty, what was going on here?

Mrs Pollenfex was going on, that's what.

I backed away slowly till I was alongside the wall again. Regaining the porch I yanked the bell pull, primed it a few times till it put up a decent fight. I expected to wait, but she was there in seconds. She must've leapt up and run. She had trouble with the door, of course. She had to walk backwards with the handle, then step aside, arms too stiff to manoeuvre. The smell was sucked out into the spring air as if it had been trapped all winter. Or was it the poem in the house, finally dying and seeding in the garden? But this poem had been sick. The smell was disinfectant from the bandages, followed by a sharp stab of tobacco smoke. And then the winter apples. I fell in love with the smells first. These were the scents of the other life. Everyone has another life, all ready and waiting for them – if they can find it. Usually you wait forty-five years, and when it comes along you're too worn down to enter it. You let it float by. You spend the rest of your life with your head in your hands. But to've found it already, when I was only seventeen!

It was all there: the whole of a better life. It was a scene from my days with Kafka and Rossetti. It was stepping through the page into an old blurred photo of the doomed. I was an exiled writer in Paris, 1925. I was a poet returned from the war. I'd come to meet the decaying actress in her mansion on Sunset Boulevard. There's no room for doubt: I was that young writer come to resurrect beauty.

I walked straight through a sheet of glass unharmed. It was no illusion. It never occurred to me earlier that she was in a parallel time. That she was trapped in a mirror. That she was really part of the doomed world I saw. And how willingly she invited me to cross over. Into that world where hands clutched straws, and lips sucked like quicksand.

Even the interior was like a stage set for the amateur dramatics. Dusty old props for *Blithe Spirit* or *The Inspector Calls* in the village hall. Old tassled lamp by a black phone. Little turret side window of leaded, stained glass. The floorboards creaking under threadbare hall carpets.

– I haven't asked your name, she said.

She hadn't asked anything. I'd just walked in, closed the door behind me and followed her down the hall towards the light. Mrs Pollenfex was expecting me. I mean, it was obvious I was the student volunteer.

There were girls at college who dressed like Mrs Pollenfex. By that, I mean I didn't wonder about her age. The difference between us seemed natural and essential. She filled my world so instantly that all former values were meaningless. She appeared to me in close-up, as if I'd always seen things from a distance. There's been no distance leading up to this. She materialized in my face. I trusted her. I'd blank myself out and say: create me. Show me.

– I'm Maxine Pollenfex, she said.

– I'm Henry. Chambers. You can call me Pisspot.

That jazz club laugh was full of smoke. She blew knowledge rings. She reeked of boredom, puked confession. She knew what it was to be ecstatic. You could see she'd negotiated her own terms with Death. I knew who she was now. My Angel of Death. She'd burned her wings off in an accident. Or the sun had melted the wax. She needed me to help her fly back to the bar. Or regain the perch from which she'd fallen.

– I can't call you Pisspot, darling. I can't call you darling, either. Henry, just wait there a second.

She went into the sun-lounge – glasshouse, whatever it was. I heard her trying to gather the paintings and I knew she wouldn't manage it. She was scuffing them with her shoe and trying to scoop them like those bloody mechanical arms in amusement arcades. One grab and they always drop. She came back and showed me the pastel smears all over her fresh bandages.

– The nurse only dressed them this morning. Promise me, Henry – don't look at the pictures. Just help me stack them up and shove them out of sight. Promise?

– Yes. I promise.

I followed her into the glass room and pretended not to look. I scooped them up, looking sideways. But I saw them, of course. And I felt them too, anti-texture, made my tongue dry and the hair on my neck stand. She'd rubbed the pastels in so hard in places she'd gone through the paper. Self-portraits, every single one. We were both our own self portraits. Doublettes, the pair of us.

– Under the sofa, she said. Just boot them. Well done. Can you make tea? No let's have coffee. Do you smoke?

The kitchen was like a giant version of gran's. Coal Rayburn, big brass tap over a square china sink with wooden draining-board. Gas hot water heater which dripped and was bound with plumber's hemp. Yellow and black checked lino. Pantry with empty shelves, a few rusty cake and biscuit tins, a bread jar, a Victorian water purifier, bare bulb hanging from an ornate plaster ceiling rose. It looked as if she was camping there. There were just a few things, and they'd obviously come with her. Jar of Nescafé, bottle of milk, sliced loaf. There was a basket still unpacked from recent shopping. Full of things I'd never eaten.

I ran some water into the kettle and lit the gas. Even this exhilarated me: we'd always had electric cookers in our house. She took her coffee black with no sugar, so I said that I did too. I carried our mugs to the sun-lounge and put hers on a folding table by the sofa with the ashtray, lighter and packet of Chesterfields. She offered me one, and struggled to flip the top back and pinch one clear.

– I'll light it myself, I said.

– No! I have to. I want to. I'm not a fucking cripple.

– What do you want me to do? I said.

– Just keep me company, while I smoke my cigarette. Tell me about yourself.

I wanted to melt into that sofa and keep the clock on 2.30, but I still had Miss Flack to go and see. She didn't actually rely on me for the shopping. It only amounted to a small tin of Chicken Supreme and four ounces of Anchor butter which Mr Grist cut and weighed from a half-pounder. She looked forward to my visits, and there was nobody else in Colonel Wade's Home to talk to. Not about that week's radio plays, the poetry programme and what I might be writing. I wasn't exactly spoiled for choice either, so it was the one time in the week I always looked forward to. I was feeling guilty already. Maxine was so beautiful, so powerful, that everything else could wait.

Telling Maxine about myself was all I'd ever wanted to do. I began with the essential Henry Chambers. Last week I'd been a Georgian who wrote Nature/ War Poetry. This week I was a Beat. We'd had that fuckin' Adonis come read his poems at college the month before. All about angels sliding down bannisters and children making up nursery rhymes. He refused to answer questions, just walked off to get the train. I followed him and stood on the platform pretending I was waiting for the London train too, plucking up the guts to tell him I was a Beat poet myself. Oh yeah? he said. I was at your recital, I said. How much did they pay you? Fifty nicker, he said. Stupid fucking poetry accent. Load of crap, he said. I'd rather be at home smoking a joint.

– I'm a Beat poet, I told Maxine.

– Really? she said, and meant it.

I could see she was relieved that I hadn't said I was a pot-holer or a Head into Hawkwind. Everywhere I went, some freak always said: wanna score some shit, man? I told her I was going to University to do English. The rest was silence, an open book. I couldn't mention Miss Flack in case she told me to run along to your old lady.

– I paint too, I said.

– I don't fucking paint, she said. That's just therapy. But this is great. Listen, hey, I write poetry.

I asked who her favourite poet was.

– Sylvia Plath.

– I've got a first edition of *The Colossus*, I said. Knicked it from Tonbridge Library.

I'd actually knicked it for someone else, but I could get it back.

– Knick some poems for me, Maxine said.

I promised I'd be in the glass case at Tunbridge Wells reference library that very evening. The Poetry Cracksman, slipping the 1891 Collected Christina Rossetti into my bag. And then I did tell her everything, in one stupified sentence. Until I'd clapped eyes on Maxine rocking in the sun-lounge, it was as if I'd never noticed the world around me. Like, you had to live somewhere, so I lived in Hawkhurst. Parents were just parents, old baggots moaning day in and day out, but they didn't matter. You just got on with the little discoveries you had to make yourself. But now all that was unbearable, being in the bum class with shameful parents at a college full of Summerhill cories.

– Poor Pisspot, she said.

– How did you hurt your arms? I said.

– I hurt them, she said. Don't worry. Come into the kitchen now.

She wanted me to cut and peel some vegetables, squeeze a lemon, butter some bread, peel an orange. She said she'd damaged her tendons and couldn't grip anything properly. I kept thinking of her rocking like that.

– I can come again, I said.

– Another week's no good to me, she said.

– It doesn't haff to be weekly. I can come tomorrow, I said, at two o'clock.

– Come for lunch, she said. 12.30. Will you? Promise?

– Yeah, I promise.

– Cross your heart and hope to die?

– Cross my heart and hope to die.

seven

I left Plato Villa at half-three, and life after Maxine began like this: an awkward tea with Miss Flack. I arrived late, left early, fending off what I'm sure were just normal enquiries. I couldn't tell her it was me who'd been sent to her niece. It wasn't meant to happen. She wouldn't understand. Miss Flack'd told me she'd had her hymen surgically removed at the age of sixty-five. But in my altered state she seemed all-knowing and interrogative. I felt like a disloyal git, already thrown off course by Maxine, already consigning Miss Flack to second best. In fact, I'd no idea what I was doing at all, or how to accommodate Maxine into my life. Ninety minutes of Maxine invalidated the whole of my seventeen years. Life was suddenly on a hat-trick.

I ran to the public library and gatecrashed a chair by the glass case upstairs. I scratched under my shirt and round my neck. I must've been growing new hair already in my hormonal upheavals. I dumped a folder on the table and pretended to write for a minute or two. I sucked the pen as if my poetry-knicking-for-Maxine thoughts were projected all over the wall saying: just need to look up that Rossetti poem in the glass case, not gonna knick it ... I tried writing one myself, my first Beat love poem to the older woman. It was worse than Benny Hill, eyes like pools, football pools, Maxine dividend, four score draws and away ... In the end, I just stuffed the fucking Christina Rossetti Collected straight in with my college folder and walked out with it. Once outside I felt untouchable in a life which was now unbearable without Maxine.

Next day at 12.30, I found the door ajar. I yanked the bell-pull and she shouted from the kitchen. She knew it was me. This made me think that I had her to myself, in the whole world. The nurse hadn't been, because Maxine's bandages were filthier than the day before. But she'd changed into one of those puff-sleeved Ophelia tee-shirts and a crumply loose skirt with Indian patterns. She smelled of primrose oil. I wore my best green loons and my crushed velvet jacket with the fascia board lapels that hung loose like folds and had three tin butterflies tabbed in formation. I suppose she knew right then what would happen. My being there was consent, but both of us dressing up ... well.

We were sitting in the sun-lounge with our salads. I hated salad, normally. Sunday dinners at home in summer were always salads with pork pie and chips. I was sick of hearing the old man say: 'Eat yer lettuce. Bill Butters give that to me.' But Maxine's salad was like a salad in an impressionist painting. It was like laying in the garden with her, or bumming round the Mediterranean. There were avocados with olive oil vinagrette, French cheese, real black pepper, capers, silver onions, Italian bread, garlic sausage, white wine, grapes and walnuts. I'd never eaten like that before. I never even guessed you could eat like that. At college I just had the savoury rissoles and beans in the cafeteria. I'd always imagined the real taste of wine from the smell of a cork I picked up from the back of a wine bar once. My soirée wine with wallaby and horse wasn't a wine at all, apparently. Just a cheap Muscat for making jam or something.

I handed Maxine the book. We were at the folding table, face-to-face, really close, eating.

– Here, I said. I stole you some poetry.

When she saw it she said:

– Oh, my God. Oh, darling.

She was out of breath, shocked and laughing.

– I can't believe you did that for me. No-one's done anything like that for me before. No-one's dared. God, it must be worth a fortune. It's beautiful. It's never been read. It's a first edition. It's ... Let me give you a kiss.

She kissed me on the forehead, a bit of lettuce stuck to me. She scooped it off with her little finger and put it back in her mouth. She swallowed me whole. We drank more wine. Soon I was just helping myself to her Chesterfields, her lighter, her wine. I asked her questions. She said I wouldn't want to know the answers, it was all too boring. Who was she? Why was she there? Where did she live? She said she might feel like telling me if she got some fresh air, so we went for a walk.

I could tell then that she had this other life I'd never be part of. It was the raincoat she put on over the hippy gear. An off-white plaid-lined Burberry. She put it on because it'd been one of those spring shower days, sweeping clouds and jagged blue skies, when even dragging on Maxine's Chesterfields was like a mouthful of spring breeze. She walked in a half-dance, hands in coat pockets, swinging the hems from side to side. She picked her way across pavings like playing tread-on-a-crack-marry-a-rat. Then she told me, when the air was fresh, the things I didn't want to know. The house belonged to the family on her parents' side. She was married to Gerald the stockbroker, and they lived off the Portobello Road in London. Her two sons were at The Gunmakers, a boarding school in Tunbridge Wells. She'd driven them down for the new term, and stayed on at the house for some peace and quiet, to write poetry. She often did, and the boys came and stayed with her at weekends. If she could cope, that was. Because – and she said, I'm sorry, Henry – because Plato Villa was where she came when she couldn't.

– Cope? I said.

It was the best I could do, question and drown. To me, she had everything. Her life was perfect, strange, different. I thought she was a true bohemian, privileged, probably famous, rich. What was there to cope with? Christ, cope with what?

– Sometimes it gets too much, you know. No, you don't, do you? Hold my hand.

Her hand was dry and strong. She squeezed mine, I felt the bandage. Now, like her, I didn't want to cope either. This wouldn't be fair. And obviously not coping was a constituent of the life I had to lead there.

– I can't cope either, I said.

– Darling, no. You've got to tell me.

She squeezed my hand again. I said it was all in my poems.

– I want to read them, she said.

At Dunorlan Park we hired a rowing boat, number 12. I rowed to the far end, under the trees. Maxine said to let it drift, and sit where she could put her head on my lap. Straight off, she felt me hard against her ear. She put her hand there to verify.

– Oh, sweetheart, she said. You do fancy me. I'm so touched.

She undid my zip.

– Fuck me! She almost shouted it.

– I want to, I said.

– I can't today. Please understand, she said. Next week, I promise.

Then I came in her mouth and she licked me clean.
– You're my first, I said.

She went back to London the next day. She said that she'd write or phone, but she wouldn't give me her address or telephone in case Gerald answered. I really couldn't cope with college any more. I just sat in the canteen and wrote Maxine poems, abandoning the Beats and regressing to Georgian and *fin de siècle*, the late nineties. Sad decay poems with rotten apples, falling leaves, French autumns, and cold seas which desired me, rushing in to sweep me off the pier, or Angels of Death who dunked boatfuls of sad poets in velvet jackets off the coast of Dieppe. Now that I was in Maxine's parallel tropic, nothing that I read made any sense at all. Revision notes congealed into academic blockage, the set books blended into one insurmountable text. I didn't wash my prick either. I kept getting it out to look at, thinking she'd been there just yesterday, the day before yesterday, three days ago, four, five, six… Where was she?

I walked past the house, but the Austin Maxi wasn't in the garage. For the first time in over eighteen months I skipped my visit to Miss Flack. I was too afraid she'd guess, or tell me her niece had moved to Scotland. I was counting on the old baggots not guessing something was up, too. For the moment it could pass for exam nerves. Chainsmoking out of my bedroom window; at half-mast all day from lack of sleep. But what would happen after the A Levels? What would happen when Maxine came back? To ME. Christ, imagine that! My beloved, right there in the front room. Would it ever be possible? No. They should never meet. Imagine it: the two-piece suite from Mr Miles' basement rejuvenated with banana-chew brown, stretch nylon covers. The old woman on the sofa folding the *Daily Express*. The dog scorching and panting on its mat, an old yellow cardie too close to the one-bar electric fire. The old man's slipper kicks it aside.

– G'worn, move yerself, dawg. Now then, Henry, who've we got here?
– This is…

She vanishes, of course, flushed out of that house like vermin. The old bag's echo rolls down the years: Too good fer you, boy.

There'd be the real years, the Pisspot years, without her instead.

41

Encounterless walks, the twice-weekly half-hour alone in the saloon
bar up the Royal Oak, sipping half a pint of ginger-beer shandy
with Son of Dust – if I ever spoke to him again. Then coming in the
shed door at 9.30pm sharp, wiping my feet, changing into slippers,
bracing myself for the old bag's inevitable remark:
  – Wet yer whistle then, boy?
  And then the bastard:
  – Where'd yer goo?
  – Up the Oak.
  – See anyone?
  – Nope.
  The A Levels were a week away. I didn't care. I could hear them
tidying up downstairs after *News at Ten*. The glass widget rattled
in the milk saucepan. Pinky was let up the back garden for her
business. The back door bolt, the ritualistic turning off of lights,
the front door latch. She always came up first, stairs creaking to
her particular pitch. The cold tap trickled lightly, the toilet flushed
in shame. The airing cupboard door squeaked like a mouse. Then,
as she opened and shut the dressing table drawers, here he fuckin'
came, the cunt, pounding up the stairs, snatching a fresh hanky from
the airing cupboard as taps gushed and the tooth-mug slammed like
a pint pot against the iron bath. Light chord yanked, the porcelain
knob ricocheted against the beading. Then darkness, and the vow
of silence slammed down on number 51. Beds creaked under cold
sheets. The absolute void again.
  That was it, wasn't it? Maxine, she'd recognized in me a void
that I didn't know existed. And it was *that* that she came after: the
Hawkhurst Void. Not me. I just carried that void, as if it was a
mystical trust that I had to pass on when the one true person came
and demanded it. And it was Her. I am come, she said. Are you the
keeper of the one true VOID?
  The truth was, I couldn't pass it on. She'd made me covet it. If
I gave it to her, she'd take it and go and I'd be alone again down
Kilner Road.

eight

Directory Enquiries said there were no Pollenfexes and they certainly would not give me the numbers of all the Pollenfexes in the rest of the world. I had no choice but to try and wheedle it out of Miss Flack. No mean feat, either. She'd been built for the war, half tank, half tweed. In her youth she'd been a Communist supporting the war against Franco, writing Irish tales for the Cornhill and publishing civil war verse in the *Observer* and *New Statesman*. In the 1930s, for chrissake. A life with few adventures, she said, the dull round of a gel having to earn her keep; the poor relation, being disinclined to marry. She'd met Yeats at Dorothy Wellesley's place. She'd been her secretary and had to follow the woman up and down staircases and in and out the toilet as Lady W dictated spasms of poetry off the top of her head. I tried reading it, but it really was a load of dandruff. Miss Flack took it all down, direct onto a portable Lion Brand typewriter which sat on a velvet cushion to protect her knees, and that was how it was published. That was what did her legs in, that woman and her verse. Miss Flack called it verse, see. Like she called stories 'tales.'

As she told me these same stories for the hundredth time, I couldn't see how I'd ever get Maxine's phone number or even her married name out of her. She still didn't seem to know it was me who'd been sent to Plato Villa. I stared at the pre-warmed china cups for help, at the milk in a yellow jug with a Devonshire scene. Maybe Maxine was in Devon.

– Where did you get this jug? I said.

– Biddeford, chum. During the war. I was on the catering side, you know, didn't have the legs for anything more stalwart...

Now and then she'd notice me and say:

– Exam nerves? Tuck into the grub, chum. If I might say so, you're looking peeky.

It was as if all this hockey stick lingo was for my benefit, just to emphasize my seventeen years against Maxine's thirty-four and Miss Flack's dozens and dozens. I even allowed myself a sense of

43

disappointment in her, because she obviously hadn't ever mentioned me to Maxine, or vice versa. Which meant that I was a private vice, and didn't transcend whatever social models or poetical tidelines the two of them had ear-marked for me. My sense of being a universal figure, Miss Flack's protegé, the poet, took a dent. It was her that signed me up for the Poetry Society too, The Tunbridge Wells Chalybeates, soon as she clapped eyes on me. She was its talent scout, see. I leapt at the chance, filling up my notebooks fast as a dog licks its dish. There was my source of self-esteem for two years, against all the co-ed tossers walking about in dufflecoats with *Tubular Bells* tucked under their arms and doing silly walks and dead parrot sketches. They read *The Hobbit* in the college canteen while I was knocking back *The Cantos* in huge gulps. Can't say the Chalybeates took to me, either. All those rose brocade sofas and biscuit dunking at half-time. Retired solicitors in black suits, spinsters in pink chiffon who buried their beloved pug every fortnight in an ode.

– Obscure, dear, they'd say when I read out my concrete haiku sequence. I wouldn't be going back there. All my poems were about Maxine now.

Me and Miss Flack did our usual poetry on the radio round-up. Ted Hughes was on Friday evening, talking about *Wodwo*. Here was a chance to get Maxine into the conversation.

– I find his imagery trite, axshully. Sylvia Plath's much more, uhm … she's got … she's a genius. No-one writes like her, do they?

Pathetic or what. She was supposed to say: My niece does. And the rest'd be Sherlock Holmes for beginners.

– I thought that pig farmer's wife was showing signs once, she said.

– She just copies anything she reads…

– Now now, Miss Flack said. I'm sure you're both on the right lines, as it were. The main thing is to keep at it.

She was sitting side-saddle on the bed with her tea, legs like bolsters. I looked round the room and took another tired bite at the cake. Eight-year-old Ireland calendars with paintings of heavy brown fields, stark horizons, winter oaks. No photos of Maxine. The Dundee cake disintegrated in my lap and I picked the crumbs up one by one.

She had the kettle on again, rinsing the cups. She pulled the window tight and soon there was steam everywhere. She straightened some egg cups she'd knocked over on the shelf.

– Sit up, boy, she said to them. Imagism's fine as far as it goes, of course.

– Imagism?

– Yes, chum. Didn't you mention the Imagists?

– No, the Confessionalists.

– Oh, boy. Colonel Wade says I get so muddled. Only the other day I heard a chap downstairs telling me he lived here and I couldn't for the life of me place him, not seeing terribly well out of my current spectacles, so I made an awful bird's nest. Poor chap was pointing to a map of County Antrim, someone having told him of my Irish connections, you see. Hmmmm, now how the devil did I get here? Oh yes. How about tales? Anything new? Yea or nay?

I said I'd written a prose-poem about … about her niece! There, I'd said it. But Miss Flack was playing to the whistle and was on another bully-off, totally skew-whiffed it. She hadn't quite connected with the right 'niece,' had she.

– Oh yes, I can see the attraction of course, to be sure. My aunts at Tring, they brought me up, you know, I'm what they call genteel – the poor relation, dear, the niece of burden. My aunts fed me Angela Brazil at what they deemed the correct age. But oh dear me, I deemed back that they would not do! Headmistresses burned them, of course, so I burned them. Fielding was my man in those days. William Brown was a character, though. Ginst kith and kin we were, me and William. William your cup of tea, Henry? You've not been made to hold wool, dear, and read *Pilgrim's Progress* to aunts with ear trumpets and lorgnettes. You're looking puzzled, chum. Have you not met William Brown at all? Or were you an Outlaw yourself? Henry, of course, is one of the Outlaws, and William was almost certainly conceived in Hawkhurst. Never mind, chum, she said. I don't expect you have time in between reading the genuine stuff, hmmm?

The letter came Friday morning. The genuine stuff. *My Darling*, it started. Maxine'd almost scratched it out, turned it into a lino-cut with a Rapidograph. Greek 'e's and 'd's, spikey black writing on a sheet torn from a student's notepad which paid no heed to the lines. It was writing which looked as if it had been composed in the dark. Writing which provoked anxiety and relief in every sentence. She said things were bloody with Gerald and he'd made her see a doctor. But she'd charmed this doctor, and got her contraceptive pill prescription renewed, specially for me. I just had to promise not to be so sad. She was spending the weekend at Plato Villa with the boys, so why didn't I come round Monday, for lunch? She enclosed some of her poems, torn from an anthology of London poets. Torn from Sylvia Plath's shroud, by the look of it. Poems like hacksaws. One began:

> *You fucked me like the moon.*
> *You made me big enough*
> *To slice.*

Every stanza had a blade, a knife, a cutter, a saw, a razor. There was blood everywhere, and yet I still clung onto my image of her slipping with that tub of boiling water. And me too, I'd dumped all that sublimity from my own poems, replacing it with a kind of poisoned rural idyll. I'd started using the word *fuck* a lot at college. Someone asked: what on earth'd got into me? Nothing, I said. Well, she said, whatever it is, you're being an idiot.

Come Monday, Maxine kissed me as soon as I was in the kitchen. Among the avocados and the Rocquefort and the Bourgogne Blanc. She took my hand and put it up her dress. She'd taken off her knickers. She pressed my finger hard against the top of her minge, all before eating. She went *ahhh* like she'd broke a rib, and wet my hand.

– See, she said. You just have to touch me and I come.

I didn't know what was happening. Apart from innocence, I didn't understand this complete abandoning of chronology and sequence. The shocking possibility that my phantasies had got it wrong, that sex wasn't part of the romantic model after all.

We ate next, and I was despondent thinking that was all the sex she meant us to have that day. I could see under one of her sleeves that she didn't have the bandages, just a wide leather arm-band with studs and buckles. She kept a Chesterfield alive in the ashtray while she ate. One chew, one drag, one swig from the wine, as if she was a mine sweeper, a mechanical digger.

– Gerald's being so bloody, she said out of nothing.

– What's he done? I said, sensing that she was trying to make me accept bad news gently.

– He wants to come down here. He suspects already.

She looked at me like the fledgeling I was, the virgin in the pack.

– I've been in love before, she said. I did tell you, didn't I?

My voice must've been cracking because she leaped forward and cradled my head.

– Sweetheart, don't. You'll wreck it. Let's just have some fun. It'll be so nice, it doesn't matter what is. You know I can't just run off with you. I've got two children, for God's sake.

– You haven't left him, then?

– I'm in space, she said. We're not completely separated, it's just bumpy … he's trying to get my children…

– I mean, I said, are you sort of coping, now?

I sensed that I'd been gathered up in abberation, that I was a distorted affair now, just a piece of space debris, a shooting star, a dumb waiter. A fucking cory to the end.

– I'm very happy, she said. This minute, right now. Wait there, she said, and she fetched some things from another room. It was like my education pack, her cast-off identity for me. John Updike's two Rabbit novels, the Neil Young albums, Joni Mitchell.

I gave her my stash, too. A rapidograph and a copy of *Ariel* I'd knicked from Goulden & Curry, but she wouldn't let me write in the flyleaf in case Gerald… She grabbed a Neil Young album and led me upstairs to a musty room with bare wooden floorboards. Her suitcase was open on the floor, with clothes trailing out like road kill. There were candles and a record player, a notebook, a clock, a bottle of whisky and a sticky glass. A jar of lithium pills, a big wooden bed with a patchwork quilt. She put the record on, drew the curtain, lit a candle and undressed me. Her own clothes just fell away. I'd envisaged laying on top of her, but she wanted me to lay down first. She sat on me and touched herself, no kissing. She was like a crow on a dead animal, her one bandaged arm behind her head, her manacled wrist twitching at her minge, and all the while Neil Young going:

Tell me why-yyyyyyyy-yyyyy
Is it hard to make arrangements with yourself
When you're old enough to repay

47

But young enough to sell...

The travel clock by the bed said 2.30. A Level Sociology was about to begin, ten miles away. A million miles away. I cried afterwards, and she smoked while kissing my face. This is where it really began. I was one of her poems, it trickled out of us, running down into the valley of death. She fucked me like the moon, too. Then disappeared again, landed on the moon, for all I knew.

Next time, the bandages were gone, though the leather tunnels through which her arms passed still left most of the flesh below the elbows visible. She was slightly ashamed. It was a hot day, so she wore a green striped tee-shirt and kept putting her arms behind her back.

– I want to see, I said.

– No, sweetheart, you don't. It won't make any difference, you won't understand.

– It wasn't an accident, then, I said.

– I did explain, she said. Sometimes I can't cope.

– Can't cope with what?

– I don't know. With Gerald, with the boys and ... with me. I can't cope with myself.

– But, I said, out of my depth now, you've got everything.

She shook her head. She wasn't doing it over me, then. I'd made her cry and she unbuckled the leather, two on each arm thrust upturned in my face, as if I was on a ghost train.

– Look, she said. That's what having fucking everything's like, okay?

A farm track up both arms, purple ruts, scab-craters, slash marks. Railway lines of stitches, ridges of mutilated, repetitive self-hatred.

– They offered me plastic surgery, she said. But I don't want it. I'll only do it again.

The rest of her was so perfect, not a sign of this disturbance. It was as if she'd located the place where it was buried, and just dug and gouged till it came out. I went to touch this battlefield.

– No, she said, snatching her arms back. I'm ugly. I don't want you to think I'm ugly.

– I don't, I said, not knowing why I hadn't, or couldn't, make her feel beautiful.

It was July, our fifth meeting. My University days were over before they'd begun. I'd made it to A Level Art, but someone put *After The Goldrush* on half-way through the afternoon. I walked out in tears and never went back, just let the proletariat down without remorse. It was always a Monday now. We were in the sun-lounge after what Maxine called 'our fuck,' which involved her kneeling on the bed, dog and bitch. She never let me see her face or kiss her. The schools broke up the following week, and she said it would be harder for her to drive down to Plato Villa. She'd have to bring the boys, and then there were people in the family who used the house for holidays or sunny weekends. Then she had to take the boys to stay with her sister as she always did, and so on. They thought she was better, so she had to join in now, friends and family. She was on medication. Oh, right, so it was the medication, not me.

– You don't want to see me, I said, and started crying. The record player was on, Simon & fuckin' Garfunkel. *America*:

And the moon rose over an oooooooopen field …

– Please don't, she said. Please, please. You don't realise how hard it is for me.

She was reading the *New Statesman*, as if she was concealing another book. I couldn't see her face either, she'd spread the pages open, crouched behind them. Her cigarette had burned halfway through in the ashtray. I was looking at the back pages from where I sat. It was as if the sun went in and a shadow slowly crept from the corners. A blood-red sun, a litmus paper. It was blood, the whole fuckin' back page was soaked. I ran round the room like a wasp behind glass.

– What've yer done? I said.

– Just leave me, okay? she said. It's the only way. Just go. I had to do it or we'll never be able to see each other again. Go on! Get out of here, she shouted. Just let me deal with it, okay?

I stood dithering and saying but … but. A shard of broken wine bottle hit the floor. I put it wet and dripping into my pocket.

nine

The baggots knew something was up now. Without college, with nowhere to go every day, they were back in my life, fraying my edges and tutting, all a short fuse to the moment when the old man clogged on my door.

– I wanna come in, Henry. I wanna talk to you…

– Free country, I said.

– Enougha your lip. Yer ma's worried sick, he said.

I could hear the old woman banging cake tins and cupboard doors downstairs so she wouldn't catch anything we said. He always blamed her indirectly or used her neurotics to get at me himself. He never said 'yer ma's getting on my wick again about some of your habits.' And she couldn't show emotion without puking up or crushing wet hankies into her eyeballs, because he wouldn't let her. It wasn't forbidden; he just went outside and oiled the lawnmower or rearranged his stack of *Exchange & Marts* in the shed.

– About what? I said.

– You know very well about what.

Well, supposing I did. The problem was how much he knew? They'd found out I flunked college quickly enough. I'd said it didn't matter, I could re-sit them, have a year off, I just hadn't been ready… She'd said nothing, just pursed her lips and sat there keeping a hold on her sphincter. The old man treated the news like a bitter draft coming under the kitchen door.

– Brrrr, yer bloomin fool.

Too numb to say anything more till now. The fuckin' dog took it worse than them, having one of her fits so bad that the old man kicked her up the garden.

– After all that flippin' trouble we went to…

Oh, what? Like how many *Cantos* had he read behind his *TV Times*?

– We wanna know what's going on, son.

– Nothin's goin' on.

– Don't fib, lad. We've got eyes and ears.

You could tell when he was cranking over the old motor of discipline. Started with calling me 'Henry,' then went on to 'son,' and when 'lad' came it was with a meaty bit of compression which told you it was about to spark into life with 'boy.' 'Boy' was on its way, in a cloud of black smoke, so you'd better start ducking behind your easel. As for eyes and ears, well that was an under-estimation. They'd got noses, hands, mouths, antennae, proboscis and claws. They rifled in my life, predicted no good would come of it, then waited for it to go wrong. Like now.

– If you think you can sit about doin' nothing all day while yer ma waits on you hand an' foot...

Hands and feet, now. When was he gonna get to what was really bothering them? My prick. I was sitting on the bed. He stood against the door as if he was warming his aching legs on it. Blocking my escape. He was going to be late for work too.

– I wanna know if you're feelin' fit. In yerself, like...

I'd left a trail of clues, hadn't I? Like piss on snow. Till the previous day, I hadn't slept since Maxine had slashed her wrist. I didn't dare go out in case the phone rang. I'd stood at the letter box from 7am onwards till the postman came. Nothing. So I'd filched a couple of the old bag's Mogadons and dropped them at tea-time. Anything was better than the night I started shaking uncontrollably at two in the morning. It went on and on, so in the end I had to call out, said I weren't well, get the doctor. The old bag phoned him, she slept like a twig snapping. He was livid, said what the bloody hell was wrong with me. She shouted upstairs: 'E wants to know what's wrong wiv yer? I'm exhaused, I said. I'd meant exhaustion, I suppose. The doctor said: so am I, and slammed the phone down. But this time the Modagon hit me like a sledgehammer and out I went. I woke up in a pool of dribble. Christ, it was like climbing out of a concrete mixer. It was dark, I had my clothes on. I didn't know where I was. I saw my college bag and folders on the floor so I grabbed them and tumbled down the stairs. I thought I was late for college. I opened the front room door and they were drinking their steaming Horlicks, sucking up their milky skins and watching the end of *News At Ten*. I just stood there and pissed my pants. It ran down into my slippers.

– Ooohh-ehhhh, the old bag said. Father, do something.

Then there was my living shrine to Maxine. The old bag must've poked her face in it and worked it out for herself. You didn't have to do A level logic to connect with the story behind that lot, all Maxine's own genuine objects, some donated, some looted. All in a box marked *M*. The John Updikes, Robert Lowell's *Imitations*. Twenty or more empty Chesterfield packets, her cigarette holder, a lock of auburn hair. Simon & Garfunkel's Greatest Hits, the Neil Youngs. A hair-slide, a yellowing copy of *The Listener* stiff and crinkled from its soaking in her blood. A cut-throat razor with her bloodstains. Assorted shards of bloody wine bottle. Her letters to me, some poems... Jesus Christ. And the old man just couldn't say it, could he, but he knew I was sitting on a letter, that all this had been about a letter I'd just run upstairs with, torn open and hardly started reading before he came fishing through the door. Once he'd got his 'boy' out, there was no stopping him. What did I care about paying my keep and getting a job and earning my way. And whatever else he said, like, was I sure I didn't need a doctor? Or his final word:

– Well yer c'n bloomin' well come into work with me today where I c'n keep an eye on yer, boy. I don't want you hangin' round this house upsettin' yer mother...

– Oh fuck off, I said, and he came for me, knocking the easel flying and saying I wasn't too old to get 'what for.' As I tried sidestepping his leathery swipes, he saw the letter and snatched it up.

– What're you hiding, boy?

– You give that 'ere; you give it back.

He held it steady, trying to read the name, so I managed to grab it and shove it down my pyjamas.

– Go on, I said, touch the festering prick that's been up a married woman.

His pay-off was pathetic.

– I'll deal with you later. Some of us've got jobs to go to...

Who gave a fig about what he'd say when he came home. Maxine was alive. She said all of this:

London, Saturday.
My Darling,

I write in haste. Please forgive me for what I am trying to do. I hope you aren't too upset or at least able to think of me without too much pain. I wanted to phone you but wouldn't have known what to say. I was so worried I phoned Aunt Flack just on the off-chance that she might have seen you. She says she hasn't seen you for weeks. Darling, please go and see her, don't give her up. She doesn't know anything, so it's quite safe. I can't write here, we're all trying to pack for Dungeness. We're going there tomorrow for a couple of days, then Gerald wants me to go to Scotland with him. I don't know. I'll write tomorrow...

Dungeness, Sunday.

Except for you I am alone and want to be that way as it is so long since I've had my own company, except for the bog! I begin to miss you dreadfully. You were right: our love is of a magical quality. Or is it that it was? What have I done to us?

I look out to an angry grey sea, grey sky and down into my grey wood. Gerald's being bloody and I don't feel strong enough to control my tears. At the moment all is uncertain. It is now more than a whole day since I was with you. I think on Dr Leopardi's advice I shall go to Scotland, but with the children, and of course Gerald (unwanted). I will let you know. Everything hurts.

Scotland, Tuesday.

Got here yesterday. You must go out, I don't think dying of love for me is very useful. Sweetheart, please remember that you have to face the outside world, you have to deal with what takes place at home. You have a future, a life to come. This, I know, has to be faced at some time or other. I am afraid, but are you strong enough to see me again? Inside the world our love has made, there is no need for self-control. All is accepted, but at home it is not. When I come back here after being with you, I feel always on my guard and very separate. Of course they don't understand you, there is no understanding, it is literally 'another world.' I have just this minute received another letter from you sent on from Plato Villa. Even though it is wonderful to read your letters, please don't send any more like that. It's too dangerous. I know it must have been so difficult... I can't explain Monday yet.

I'm still explaining it to myself. But it wasn't serious, so please don't panic. I'm just so glad you aren't angry. It was a beautiful letter. I never expected it, it was such a surprise. I'm sorry I can't write like you. As for seeing you, it would probably be just as easy or easier. As yet, I have no fixed date to see Dr Leopardi, but when I have it will be no trouble getting away on my own. And yes, darling, I did tell him about you, I had to or he can't really help me. His remark about you 'emotionally masturbating' was cruel, I know, but he's said many such things to me. That is why, in an odd way, I like him. I don't know, sweetheart, I feel too close to get it in focus properly, but perhaps as in so many similar remarks he has made to me, there is some truth.

The post here is archaic, it sometimes takes four days to collect from this point, so I write in haste to get this to you asap. I still don't understand how yours came here. There is only one callbox and I don't think your parents would accept a transfer charge call from Scotland, and ten pence would only last a few seconds. I love the way you write, at odd times, like a diary. It makes me feel so near you. Up here is so beautiful, almost too much, the mind cannot digest it. All the hills are heather covered, and the river sounds in my ears all the time. Things between me and G are calmer, or rather stagnating politely. It's quite warm considering summers here, very bearable. Gerald's business up here will I hope soon be over, so I can be much nearer to you in London.

This afternoon I took a bath, then lay naked in front of the open fire. All afternoon. There was no-one here. They had all gone to Edinburgh and I was, by choice, supposed to cook. But laying there reminded me so much of us. With my usual lack of self control I ached and hurt and so longed for you. I shut my eyes and dreamed of us together. (When will it be?) Then I re-read your letters and poems.

Later… It is difficult to write here now, surrounded by people. That is why you get these grubby pages from my notebook – it's easier to close! This letter must go, so then must I. Please sweetheart, be positive, be strong and face the more restrictive atmosphere of so-called normality. Think about going back to college, you musn't waste all that talent.

Be careful, please, I don't want you hurting too.

After dinner, 8.15.

Darling, I just want to tell you I love you. I did not send this letter as it would not go till tomorrow anyway. I now feel very revived and clean though still aching for you to be inside me with the sweetness of all that spring rain in the garden. O sweet, I shall worry about you at home unless you get away. You must remember they do not understand and never will. People are very unaware. Curiosity is not interest, but an excuse for lack of other interests. I wish I could protect you. You are very truthful when you write and do not, I think, act (unless you feel like an avalanche). Enclosed heather.

I've had two beautiful letters from my children. They're so sweet. I wish I could have them as my own entirely without G claiming half all the time. He is slowly turning them against me, even at so young an age.

All my love, darling
Maxine XXXXXXXXXX

ten

We all gathered outside the Baptist Chapel on a Saturday morning mid-August, 9 o' clock sharp for an early fag and a stick of Wrigleys, to march on the Manse for the Parson Dust Revival or whatever it was: the Parkinsons Show, Sooty's Last Bow. It was his birthday, fifty, according to Son of Dust. My old man was fifty too, but he didn't have snot coming out of his ears and jaws like castanettes and veins like chicken feet sticking in his face, even if he was a cunt.

Son of Dust invited me himself, me and everyone the Parson'd ever said hi to. He told me it was the inaugaral annual Parson Dust Ramble, that stout shoes or walking boots were recommended, and to bring a packed lunch. He didn't mention the little gig that takes place under the Parson's window first, where he's wheeled onto the balcony by Delilah Dust in her blue polka dot apron. The Parson must've had the embalmer working on him since dawn. The rouge blush, the egg box in his cheeks, a dark red dressing gown over the striped suit he must've worn at Bible college. When his mouth twitched I thought we'd come to see a miracle. Mother Dust said: Look everyone, he's smiling. Then Brim Stone was supposed to strum on a guitar craftily hidden for the occasion behind the rhododendrons. Only Son of Dust, who didn't know better, who couldn't even play the automatic harp, had put it out the night before. His reason was understandable, according to others. Me, I couldn't see why anyone would fuss over their old dodster's birthday, enough to round up half the nutters in the village to come catch his dribble under the balcony and smell his farts which came outside with him for some fresh air. Son of D. hadn't wanted to leave anything to chance apparently, that's why he'd put the guitar out at night. Light rain, heavy dew. Brim Stone picked up his pride and joy, all set to sing *Morning has Broken,* and it unfolded into seven pieces and played *Morning Has Broken It* instead. Surreal or what. The bridge and strings trailed on the ground like one of those clothes lines you stretch over the bath. The sides fell off to reveal a music-coffin. Brim's left holding the neck. The glue was soluble, you twat. I wasn't the only one with a burst water main either. Even Daughter of Dust was sniggering like a bag of jelly.

– Oh shit, Brim said.

So we all sang dry, a ditty Brim Stone composed: *Happy Birthday praise the Lord, for Parson Dust has grasped the sword, of age.* Sounded like Crosby, Stills, John Wesley and Young.

On Maxine's advice I was being outward bound, you see. I'd done Miss Flack, and now I was doing pride and joy. Everything would be fine after all. Maxine loved me and that was all that mattered, that was all the wheels needed to turn and get me out of Hawkhurst. Maxine was coming in four days time and we were going away together. Yes, I was going to spend a whole night in bed with her. Maybe if she could just fix things a bit I'd be getting out of that dump for good after all. In the meantime, there was no harm in seeking company among the 'unaware,' as Maxine called everyone but us, enjoying the summer with a few Christian rambles.

Son of Dust showed a bit of his old self too and sang a proper song to kick us off: *I got ramblin, I got ramblin orn ma mind...* There were twenty-five of us at the muster, rambling towards Bodiam. Parson Potter was captain in his fell boots, brown cords tucked inside his chunky socks, walking stick with leather thong, ordnance survey in a plastic bag hanging round his neck on a boot lace, yellow windcheater, box of emergency flares, space blanket, morse code machine, fucking army biscuits... God was just good for bumming money and petrol then, not for asking the way or telephoning a rescue helicopter. I knew this footpath blindfold.

Parsnip Potter was dressed identically to him in her recto verso. Same yellow face, as if neither of them had stepped outside the vestry door in years. She had their victuals in a brand new rucksack God had left outside their backdoor last night. Son of Dust hadn't stopped to ask how come God acts like a mail order catalogue for one parson while allowing the other parson to languish into a vegetable. Still, I'd come out of evolution and got Maxine. I was in love, and bursting at the seams. I had to tell someone the Good News today. Maxine's letters were pouring down. I had a new one in my pocket to re-read at first refreshments. Came that morning:

Darling one,

I am in bed alone, the tape is playing and I'm remembering the time our bodies first touched in the rowing boat. Now here, I look back with nostalgia, and because of you, and only that, I wish I wasn't so well this week, and then nobody would want me here with them and I'd be nearer you. Did we not snatch such moments of happiness out of those grey days? Each moment brings back to me some thought or memory and makes a small silent pain and longing. (Darling, you would laugh, I've just caught myself stroking the unlit cigarette in my holder).

People must think I'm really crazy. I write saying I'm well again then rave about the wonderful time I had when "sick and alone" at Plato Villa. Does it not strike you as very odd, with strange intention, in all our moments of beauty nothing ever interrupted them, we were always so completely alone and together?

Later... Sweetheart, you grew for me such wonderful happiness out of such a dark, gloomy world. I hope I did the same for you. I tried, and gave to you not because I wanted to give, but to give all I had made me happy. All I had – it is still yours.

Goodnight love, my darling one...

We'd got as far as The Moor on the edge of Hawkhurst. Dust's new bird had her sister with her, sixth former at TWIGGS, Tunbridge Wells Girl's Grammer School.

– I'm Lucy, she said. Are you the poet?

I knew the smile, the teeth. The portcullis soon comes down, dropping as her jaw would drop. All the girls at college had been like her. Lucy was a bit more neurotic, maybe. Eyebrows raised, she stopped walking. I stopped too. She was wearing a wide-brimmed straw hat with a daisy chain round it, white calico smock, long flowered dress of Laura Ashley fab, and her geography field trip boots. Just for the record, I too had walking boots. My cherry-wood cane, green haversack with a flask of black Maxine coffee, bread and cheese, an apple, Smith's crisps and a Bar Six.

– Can you keep a secret? she said.

– What?

– I've got some paki-black. Have you got a straight?

– I've got a couple, I said. Can you keep a secret?

– Yes, she said.

– Well, I'm having an affair with a married woman ... her name's Maxine. She's ...

– Well, Lucy said in a high-sprung voice that was a bit Flacky, I'm not pregnant, anyway. And off she ponced, god knows why. She knew how to steal a moment.

– Maxine's not pregnant? I said, hopping after her.

Parson Potter nearly heard that.

– Keep your voice down, Lucy said. It's me who's *not* pregnant. I just found out. I had to tell someone ...

Jesus Christ. So she told me as we lingered at the rear. Just after her exams she'd been hitching back from Tunbridge Wells. A travelling electrician from Bromley, or so he said. Married, loved reading. Silent but pretty wife. Screwed Lucy in the back of the van. Poor Lucy, wanted a craftsman, a soiled-but-honest artisan wiping his tools on a William Morris leather apron. She wanted to be had in a haybarn, *The Virgin and the Gypsy*, wild breasts in the rain, barefoot over the farmyard. The back of his van smelled of wires, her head lay on a screwdriver. His jeans were round his ankles and he had to tell her to bend her legs open or he couldn't get in. She said she ended up squashed against his tool bag and kept grabbing monkey wrenches as he made her dress all oily. The smile was gone. She gave him her phone number but he never rang. I couldn't tell her about Maxine then, and she didn't ask. I had something which went beyond her range, here. For instance, on Friday I'd got this:

Edinburgh, Wednesday.

Darling one,

I wish we were together in an old haunt. I enclose a book of Christina Rossetti. I had it as a child and loved it. It must have originally been an aunt's or something as I see the name and 1912 in the front, who are my relations and related to Shelley. When I look it seems the poems and passages I marked when young I could not have known the meaning of, or realised what they would mean later, considering what has happened. How are you? I miss miss and miss you, every way, every day. Perhaps tomorrow when I get back from

Glen Lyon I will hear. There I can write more easily. Here
we are staying with a business friend of G's. Your letters are
always close to me but your memory closer still. Soon we
shall see one another.
Love, my darling one,
M.

So, Lucy's sister was Son of Dust's new-chick-on-the-ramble. I
don't know how he did it. He got the pick of TWIGGS, stunners,
Gothic ineffables, and now a flapper, Jerry from Cranbrook, just
like William Brown's sister Ethel. Floppy white sun hat, hooped
day-glo tights with a tartan skirt just above her knees, bumper
boots and long mousey hair falling over one of these delicate faces
Son of Dust seemed to go for. I could see why too, looking at his
family. They'd all got lips like rolled up carpets and Parson Dust
had shrunk till all that was left was a nose in a dressing gown.
Delilah Dust looked like those big hens in Beatrix Potter books,
the ones dressed in bonnets and aprons waddling to market with
a basket full of eggs. She was like that on the ramble, bringing a
basket with all their sandwiches wrapped in checkered hankies and
cutlery strapped into pairs with their names on. Seaside Dust had his
orange windcheater and a compass round his neck and a field guide
to British Birds. He'd got feet like skis and a nose like a streetlamp
too. Shove a bulb up it and it would've lit half of Hawkhurst. He'd
be seven feet when he got to my age.

Parson Potter insisted we say grace before tucking into our picnic.
He made us sit in a circle round him and Parsnip. Apparently God
provided my Smith's Crisps in the same batch as his sliced hazlitt
and farmhouse loaf, which looked curiously like one of Baldock's
loaves, and left God looking like a shoplifter now. During grace I
had plenty of time to scan the congregation. There weren't many
of us with our eyes open not mumbling 'amen' and saying 'verily'
and 'you said it, Parson.' One of the atheists was Jerry the flapper.
She looked as bored as his other chicks when it came to worship.
This made it even more inexplicable. What did they get out of it?
He couldn't have renounced lewdness and hash after all, if these
chicks were born-agains just to be with him. So I decided to tell
him about Maxine when I got the chance.

Wasn't till we were almost back in Hawkhurst that Son of Dust lingered a pace for me to catch him up. He put his arm round me and patted me on the back.

– Hen, man, I'm really touched you came along today. It's been, wow, great, truly cool. Tell me how it's going, Hen. What's the buzz?

– I'm not going to university any more... Er, having a year or two off. I don't think formal academic slavery is the way to release my potential.

– Oh, Hen, in a way I'm sorry to hear that. Will you find some labour?

– I'm pretty occupied, axshully... I'm having an affair with a married woman.

Fucking aida, you should've seen him. Glimpses of Parson Dust in his face, the Devil-Buster going off in his ears.

– I'm mightily sorry to hear that, Hen. I really wish you hadn't told me. It's kind of ... it's kind've spoiled my day, if I may say so. That's a wicked thing to be proud of, yeah? I don't wanna hurt your feelings and that, but man, I think you've let the devil dwell in your heart too long. I'm not being rude, but I don't wanna walk with you no more.

When I got in the two baggots were sitting there like a tray of ice cubes watching Des O' Connor sing *Give me the Moonlight*, their favourite song under normal circumstances. There was a letter on the table, nothing else. Pale blue envelope surrounded by a sea of daily furniture polish. Addressed to me. Maxine's handwriting. I nearly puked up God's Bar Six.

– Whass siss doin 'ere? I said. There ain't two posts on a Saturday.

The old woman's voice had three stars and a picture of a frozen fish in it.

– Came s'mornin. Postman forgoddit. 'E gave it t'yer father after you left, boy.

I ran upstairs nearly crying. I knew they'd fuckin' read it. You could see it'd been steamed open. The old man'd got a business on the side steaming open letters in his shed up the back garden. It was linked to the kitchen by an old pink intercom the dentist give him. The shed was full of alternators, dynamos, distributors. The ratbag pressed the button over the kitchen sink and you could hear

his blow-dried voice rise above the crackle.
– Yes, ma?
– 'Nother one o' that floosy's letters to steam open, father...

Pevensey, Friday.

Love,

I've done your trick and taken too many tranquilisers, so I've come outside to write in a wind that would awaken the dead. I am going to start writing again. I must. It is perhaps selfish to desire self-expression, but it makes me more livable with, and makes me also able to live inside myself. I enclose the stupid letter I wrote to you last night. It's rather nauseating melodrama which was I think induced by the Mogadon and strong whisky I had on my return...

...I hope all goes well at home today. We are so near now. Please eat sensibly and take the pills I'm sending at the right time. You will never be free to use your mind, create, write, think, work things out etc. if you are imprisoned within the sordid discomforts of your own body. I know you have this romantic idea of consumptive poets, but darling, most of their writing was done before, and the ones that managed to attain mind over matter stand out, that is why we all know them, and who knows: their genius may have been more prolific if they had the gift of physical health. My mother had consumption/TB. It just meant staying in bed for a year on yet more drugs, and the symptoms were anything but romantic! Why do I always lecture you? Sorry, but I care. Unless an emergency occurs, I won't ring Tuesday, we will meet as arranged. G is here you see, must dash to the post. Till Wednesday darling, I can no longer wait without going half crazy.

Keep well for me.

M.   X

eleven

Our venue was Tredegar, this half-weatherboard, half-brick and timber house in Newenden where these friends of Maxine's lived. She was watching out for me, came running up the lane when I got off the bus. She looked plain: jeans, red pumps, white tee-shirt with green hoops, hair tied back as if she'd just hung the washing out, like the months had worn the glamour off. But it was deliberate, she hadn't wanted to arouse Gerald's suspicions. We cried into each other's arms. I couldn't believe it – neither of us could.

Till then I'd felt okay, if a bit top heavy and nervy with excitement. I'd taken the amylchlorate like she'd said, to get a good night's sleep, then dropped the Yellow Perils a bit early at breakfast. I just didn't want it to go wrong, it was our first whole day and night together. I thought it might be a trial run, that if it went well it would become regular, till the day we'd live together in one of her cottages. So I'd swallowed all six Yellow Perils and lit up a Dunhill. Then realised all six were supposed to be staggered over the twenty-four hours. The tumult of our meeting, the crying on the guts, put a knot in my stomach and the next fag made my mouth taste like a public slash-house.

We sat at a wooden table under an apple tree out back. The field sloped down to the river, slow muddy bends full of bream. It was our most wonderful moment, we were free, it was our engagement, the Pre-Dip in Honeymoon Studies. Haystacks, swallows, the breeze scratching through the August leaves, the ripening fruit swelling on the vines, the branches, the hedgerows. We drank chilled wine, clinked glasses, kept saying: I can't believe it, neither can I, I'm so happy darling, so am I... It was a taste of life to come. I couldn't see any other outcome, couldn't imagine it had an ending or that it wouldn't loop round every summer and keep us floating, migratory lovers.

Our host Melissa was inside with a visitor. The French windows were open and I could hear voices, the snick of a lighter, the clunk of a heavy drinking glass. Maxine said we'd been given the big

63

room by the stairs, but we'd have to wait till later. Holman was out for the afternoon but due back at tea-time. I was leaning back in my deckchair holding Maxine's hand, the knot in my stomach moving upwards and turning to a lump in my throat. My eyes were blurring in and out of focus. The drowsing of bees was intermittently soothing, then raucous, like a dentist's drill. Every other feeling began to follow this pattern of uncertainty. When Melissa came out I was starting to panic. I couldn't feel my teeth. Maxine stood up.

– Melissa, meet Henry.

Melissa had a glass of red wine and a fag on the go, both in the same hand. She squinted against the sunlight and flipped her shades down over what looked like two swollen black eyes. Even in the heat her hand was cold and pudgy as we shook. She put her arm round me and went all conspiratorial. I thought she was going to lay down the extra-marital sex rules of the house. But no, something worse.

– Bit of an embarrassing thing, lovers… Her voice was slurred and bumped on a fat tongue. Henry, there's someone in the lounge you don't want to meet, so if you need the toilet or anything, go in the front door. Maxine'll show you.

– Who is it? I said.

– A colleague. John Fitzpatrick.

I must've looked blank. I needed to sit down anyway, another fag had turned my mouth more putrid than before.

– Swattenden, she said. He's recognized you.

Fuck a duck, fascist Fritz was there. She was a teacher too? Was she shagging him, then? Was this why she'd so easily consented to hosting Maxine's affair? Or was it wife-swapping and Maxine was going to shag Fritz after me? All those John Updike novels she'd given me – it was just like that, sophisticated grown-ups cruising from bed to bed… Maxine was being so cool and steady. I'd never seen her with other people, so confident, always knowing what to say. Even the boozy banter between her and Melissa went over my head. And I did need the toilet. Something in me needed to come out but I couldn't tell if it'd be snot, ear-wax, tears, piss, shit, spunk, blood or puke. Maxine kissed me outside the toilet door and reminded me to come back out via the front. The kiss, the kiss I'd waited months for, and it was hateful. It didn't turn my insides over because they were already immune to love, churning like a concrete mixer, this lump in my throat cancelling out the whole world's happiness. Nothing happened in the toilet. I looked normal, except my pupils. Then I tried to piss and saw my prick had shrivelled up to the size of a baby's finger and the foreskin was glued together tight at the tip. The piss backed up till it burst out all over the fucking bathroom wall, soaking the inside of the cabinet because someone had left the door open. I mopped it off then stuffed the avocado-coloured towel to the bottom of a wicker basket. I just wanted the lump in my throat to go, come out or descend. It had to be a real lump, like the stone over Jesus's tomb. Then I'd be free to recommence the best day of my life, my resurrection. Maybe water would shift the stone. I guzzled pints out of the washbasin tap, warm dental flush water that tasted of aluminium and bloated my guts like the knot inside was now an island. The lump stayed put. Going back through the house I saw a white Sunblest on the kitchen table. Maybe two slices of that might catch on the lump and I could swallow it. Wadding the unbuttered slices like jamrags down my throat only made it worse. I could hear Fritz through the serving hatch.

– You know what Ted Raynor always used to say?

– No, John. I never had the pleasure.

– Ho-ha-hoo. He always said if you teach them drama they'll just act up. It's a subject without disciplines.

– Oh, for Christ's sake, John, I've achieved more than that in two years.

– At some cost.

– School and drink are seperate causes, you know that, John.

– I do, Melissa. You don't have to make a come-back. Just pick up the pieces and it'll all fit into place …

I couldn't resist just easing the serving hatch open a crack. And there he was, twirling a sherry in an armchair, pale blue Saturday casuals, smoking an Embassy. What if I charged in and had my say to the man who'd conspired to keep me from books? And what could I have said? Exactly. All that was left. I'm having an affair, you fascist, with that grown-up woman sitting outside.

– Really, Chambers? You silly boy. Go and wash your hands at once …

Maxine took my hand again when I sat down.

– Darling, I was worried. Are you okay?

– Er, just a bit woozy. Let's have a walk.

– No, I think we should wait for Melissa. Your teacher will be going soon.

Most of that evening was a fragment, an excrutiating memory, as if now and again I came to during an amputation without anaesthetic. Maxine knew Melissa from a clinic where they'd been in-patients. Melissa was supposed to cook supper. Fritz left in his soft top Triumph Herald like Captain Scarlet on leave. By tea-time Melissa was locked in the bog and slogging on a wine-box. Another one with everything who called it nothing. Woken up in her dream cottage. Timber floors, beams, leaded windows, tile-hung gables, Davey lamps, inglenook, Afghan dog with obsessive-compulsive disorder, Welsh cat, more boys at public school, Citroen Dyane, rolls of pound notes in her fat purse and Holman, a husband as gentle and funny as Gerald was bloody and vengeful. Holman was an enormous man, drove a brown Granada. I liked him, I wished he was my father. Fat boy's face, chortled and pipped every remark with a joke in a gentle, beautifully mannered accent which rolled round his mouth like a gobstopper.

Melissa's one brief appeerence that evening was to fall down the last three creaking stairs then sit on the floor cracking up in front of us. Broken veins on her face, bitten nails, a fat neck she pretended to strangle with a gold chain. She had an awful hair cut. She was only thirty, and went in for perms like my old woman. She delivered a maudlin monologue on the floor, quoting Dylan Thomas then begging Maxine to tell her that Holman was a bastard, that he was wrong when he said she wasn't his intellectual equal. She could quote the whole of Hamlet,couldn't she? Her hair had gone silver from boozing.

– I've still got good legs, haven't I ? she shouted.

Holman stood wearily, looked at me and said:

– I do apologise for the depressing nature of my wife's hospitality, Henry. Maxine's no stranger to it, but that doesn't excuse it. Let's get you upstairs, Melissa.

Ten minutes later I was upstairs too, retching into the bedroom basin. Maxine held my hand throughout. I said it was indigestion, even though we hadn't eaten yet, and I lay on the bed packing in the liver salts. Maxine and Holman ate alone, now and then checking on their respective sick ones, hoping one of us might come down and perk up. The candles burned to stubs and Holman suggested we called it a day. Melissa had locked him out the bedroom.

– It might be wise if you stayed some other night, Holman said, Melissa not being herself, and Henry obviously in some kind of upheaval or downward spiral, Brewer's Droop notwithstanding.

It was then that Maxine laughed. Laughed and laughed. I was upstairs with the door open, sunk face in the black cups of my hands. They were laughing at me, at my pitiable exposure. There would be no life together, no second chance either. I'd ruined everything. She drove me home. We were silent. I was still burping from indigestible sludge in the pit of my stomach, laying on the back seat. Then the car did a neuro turn and Maxine cried out:

– I can't stand it, Henry. It's fucking unbearable.

We were hurtling down a lane the other side of Bodiam now. I propped myself up and saw the headlights swinging over hedgerows and hop gardens. She bumped us up a track on the Guiness farm, switched off and scrambled over the back seat on top of me. We clung and fumbled and kissed. I heaved and belched but my prick swelled up in her mouth. A mad farmyard screw on the back seat, shivering as our backs touched the clammy, cold plastic upholstery. She had me over and over till I crawled for the door handle, fell out and puked on all fours. Maxine rubbed my back, completely naked both of us, crying under that delicious smell of hops and honeysuckle. Then she drove me home, dropping me off in the village, as if I'd been sleepwalking and had just woken up. The baggots were in bed. Thinking I'd be out all night, they'd bolted the doors. The old man let me in, moaning like the wind through a broken window.

– Bloody hell, Henry, I'm damned sick of your shennanigans. Look at the bloody state of yer! Now get to bed and be quick about it.

I pulled the blankets over my face. She was still on her way home over the marsh and we were apart again, ripped apart this time. I whispered her name over and over.

Dungeness, 12.30 midnight.
    Darling
    I drove home dazzled by the oncoming lights, past the

places where we had been, the road by the hotel where we turned off, the bridge where only a single car can cross, the river, the signpost to Hawkhurst. And whatever has happened, the sweet retrospect of the day flooded back and I was overcome by our pain and longing. It is how we are. It will always be pain and longing. Then I was gone, away to Dungeness where the fires of the coast lights blazed orange in the dark, then home to the unceasing crash of the waves.

I am so sad for Melissa and feel so helpless for us all. All three of us escape or have done so: alcohol, pills, what does it matter? The end is the same, a deadening, a search for oblivion. Why is life so unendurable, or we so unfit to live it?

I have taken four Mogadon and a glass of whisky. I twiddle the knobs of the radio drawing forth fodder for the pain that I must always search out, a mental masochism. A tune is being played, *Un Homme et Une Femme*. Once, in love with someone, it meant so much. Now the memories are as musky as dead petals crushed between the pages in my mind.

There is no real truth between us or any human beings, nor communication. Love is only the compulsive search that always looks like ending. It never does, so love dies, and we die with it. It cannot last, we are forever shut inside ourselves. Is that what we try to escape from, the self-imprisonment? There is only one way to achieve it. Somewhere beyond is a world where no-one hurts you.

twelve

Hawkhurst on a Wednesday afternoon was a hibernaculum of silent houses, empty lanes. The traffic lights stuck on red for half an hour. Solitary figures took flowers up the cemetery, shopkeepers pottered behind blinds or down the shed. Widowers, Rotarians, British Legionnaires, the lollipop woman and the district nurse. Puppet-town. Bill Deedes the MP. Patience Strong, the poetaster, lived up at Four Throws. So did the bloke who played Robin Hood, and the TV critic for the *Daily Express* lived in The White House with Lonnie Donnegan's step-daughter lodging there as a day-girl at Lillisden. Malcom Muggeridge dossed in the next village. Roger Daltry further out, Burwash way. Hawkhurst was for the losers then, but it could never be the same again. This was the day Maxine came to Hawkhurst, when it all started going horribly wrong.

Soon as I knew she was coming, I thought I had to clear the way, polish the pipes, make sure the coast was clear. The old woman'd been shouting at me all week.

– WHAT'S SHE DOING TO YOU, BOY! SHE DOESN'T WANT YOU! SHE DOESN'T NEED YOU!

And the old bastard gunning me down in the front room while the bag shut herself in the toilet.

– Is this true, boy, that you're messing about with a ... I can hardly bring meself to say it.

– Yes, I said. I'm having an affair with an older woman. She's got...

– I don't wanna bloomin' know and yer c'n keep yer trap shut round yer ma. You better know what you're doing cause we're not gonna pick up the pieces. Heaven knows what people are saying about us. Don't you dare have the gall to bring her anywhere near here, either. No, you don't think do yer...

Blah fuckin' rhubarb. Same old wax cylinder coming down my ear trumpet.

Then, on top of all this, there were all those stray humiliations to chase off or round up for the used memory pound. I was scared of

Maxine coming there. Scared of what she'd see and how she'd react to it. To me, all the worthlessness was too visible, the baggots its joint curators. I set off on the walk I thought we'd do, just to check for potential damage. Just stepping out into Kilner Road, and there was the abyss waiting to swallow her up. A plane droned in a grey sky and my balls were like walnuts in clingfilm. Hector Haunt, old Ma Aids, all the slags' mums in curlers with their stockings rolled down, hanging out grey sheets and drip-dry shirts. I only got as far as the top of the road where a slope of brambles disappeared in long flat yellow grass and ragwort. Copt Hall. Under the brambles there used to be a big house, Copt Hall, demolished three years before when the council purchased it.

All my childhood it'd stood there. We'd called it 'the big 'ouse.' It dominated our boundary. My first real sense of it connected me with the social scale. Like when we came home from the Sunday drive to Nan and Grandad's, after seeing all my aunts who kept their front parlours locked till Sunday and scrubbed their outside toilets raw with Jeyes Fluid, perishin' cats' doodahs on the rough cinder paths, aunts who washed their grey bedsheets in the kitchen sink Sunday dinnertimes while my cousins swore and scuttled round in the dirt of bare backyards eating sugar sandwiches. Uncles were down the boozer, or resting up after plummeting from the scaffolding or getting nipped by the dustcart again. The old bag's whole family bar Auntie Beryl lived in the same road. Kitchener Avenue, grey, skin-grazing pebble-dash, dark green doors, lino kitchens reeking of coal gas and tar soap. In the front room, Grandad lived in a square-yard world, three-quarters deaf and blind outside it. He sat twelve feet away from the racing on the telly with the sound on full. All the knick-knacks on the top jigged about till they fell off, usually on the home straight when the commentator started shouting. Grandad rolled his braille fags non-stop, lungs like copper boilers. In his eighties, too, after a lifetime stoking on the tugs. One drag on an Old Holborn banger, five minutes hawking into the kitchen sink like a donkey without spewing. Then out he came and I was pushed in front of him. Pale and sacrificial while they all shouted: IT'S HENRY, ALF! Ello cocker, 'e sez. Giss a smacker, then...

On the drive home I'd lay on the back seat staunching it till we got to the top of the road and it was all right. I'd sit up, see the big house, way beyond the limits of my understanding. How could anyone live in a house that big?

– Who lives in that big 'ouse, Dad?

That would make the old lady starch up. When we parked the car she'd yank me out by the wrist and spit on her hanky, rubbing the spit on my dirty face and round the corners of my mouth. Bird bath and eye wash she called it.

– If I ever let you out t'play again, she said, juss you stay down 'ere in sight o' the front gate, you 'ear? Doan want you showin' us up.

The older I got, the further up the road I was allowed. Then the old man took over the urgent, woe-betides. The facts of life:

– Juss keep out that field, or blow me, boy!

The house fell vacant for years. Kilner Road kids reclaimed the field as common land till PC Wyman put a stop to it one summer. The Hall was let. Gardeners came and mowed and tucked. The tennis court was turfed and rolled. Two English families took up residence, fleeing from Kenya after Independence. The Hazels and the Montagus.

From then on the copse and hedges became nested and peep-holed with faces from 'down the road.' There were delicious goings-on to spy at. These people lived in a Colonial time-warp, a Richmal Crompton summer. Languid bronzed beings lounged in tennis whites. Beautiful girls in exotic frocks and olive skin, men like explorers in hunter's khaki and tropical flannels. There were rites and customs and drinks trays too strange to be believed. Unless you looked at the pictures in those Christmas Annuals, tales from Africa. White Hunter. Jungle Beast. The Flying Doctor.

I was only allowed as far as the Cow's Gate. To see anything of this spectacle I had to stand three bars up and crane my neck for a distant glimpse with toy binoculars. Here, one hot July afternoon, I met Tancred Montagu.

I was sitting on the gate sucking grass, just gazing at the house two hundred yards off. A boy my age sneaked up and grabbed me by the ankles.

– Got one, he shouted. Are they all your friends in the bushes too? My father says you lot are worse than niggers. Much worse than a bunch of ruddy Kyukes.

He was more amused than threatening. He was used to black houseboys in shabby clothes, not little white boys. I was in my let-them-down clothes, darned elbows, grass skid marks and shoes flapping their jaws. This boy was a glossy advert, son of Daktari with his chestnut hair, glittery blue eyes, firm sun-tanned face. His knee-length shorts were tight against his legs like foreign boys in French films we saw on telly at teatime. *Emile & The Detectives* or that sop with his balloon. He cast his spell on me and knew it. He was the fruit my old folks said was forbidden. He was Maxine before her time.

– I'm Tancred Montagu. Who are you?

– Enry Chambers.

– Do you live down there?

– Year.

– Show me your house. You lot spy on us, so it's a fair swap.

My best dreams begin with this bit. Floating down the road with a fortune or great news, the perfect anything, the Maxine.

– Ziss one, I said. And all my nightmares began with this bit. We stood outside my front gate looking at the semi-detached brick house with concrete porch identicle to the other hundred. Tiny lawn, chicken-wire fence. Every five years the council painted the front doors either blue or pale green. The old lady was on the prowl and saw us. Front door flew open.

– Whass goin' on? Whatyer starin' at, smirky?

She stomped down the garden path all housecoat, rolled sleeves and bunions.

– Ooz the kid wivyer?

I was still proud, and smirky Tancred wasn't scared of her. He'd stood on his Kenyan doorstep and quelled native uprisings. He'd shooed lions away from the dustbins and chased off thieving great nannys. When the old lady twigged this it would be different.

– 'E lives in the big 'ouse. I'm showin' 'im our 'wn.

– Oh, *are* yer now! Well smirky, yer c'n clear back off up yer own way.

The gate slammed behind me and I had to frogleg over smacks to my shirt tail. Tancred would save me yet, wouldn't he? Like he'd say something special, get himself invited in. He was my mate.

– Nah Mum, listen, ask 'im summing 'bout Africa ...

He opened his mouth all right, a little silver fountain of spite calling us all the names under the African sun. Then he bobbed away, a flash of laughing-white sprinting up the road. The old lady had to have the last word on it. It pleased her to have the line drawn for me. It saved her the bother of having to explain it when I was older. Like, instead of me asking where do babies come from, one day I'd ask: where does social inequality, misery and depression come from, Mum? Well, it comes from up the fuckin' road. Comes from all the big 'ouses. Yeah, so. Night-night Tancred, that was you out the picture.

– See 'ow much 'e thought o' you, the old lady said. Now ged inside an' forget 'im.

There was still a hole in the ground where Copt Hall stood. About the same size hole Maxine was about to put in our lives.

She drove to Hawkhurst in her maroon Austin Maxi. I was standing there at the bus station when she pulled up. That way, no-one would see us and I could get us out of Hawkhurst. I thought we could go for a drive, picnic on a rug. Then we'd take our clothes off, but she didn't want to. She'd really never seen inside a council house.

– Please, darling, she said. Show me your bedroom. I must see it, I must have you in it.

The old bag was in the kitchen, she didn't know Maxine was coming in.

– Ere, whass goin' on, ooze that...

But she didn't need to ask who. The Tancredometer needle was in the red.

– You shouldn't be here, she said to Maxine. You shouldn' really be 'ere at all. You're a married woman. I won't have it, waltzing into my kitchen ... get out!

– Oh, keep yer wig on mum, I said. We only want a cup of tea...

– That's right, Mrs Chambers. I'm parched. I've no intention of outstaying my welcome...

She was beaten by the accent and sulky as she filled the kettle. We all sat in the front room sipping tea as if we were bomb disposal defusing dangerous liquid. The old baggot was guard dog, dinner-lady, chaperone, moral copper, social class ombudswoman. Maxine had jeans and a rose tee-shirt with no bra, twelve-bore nipples aimed at the china dogs on the mantlepiece. The baggot just sat shuffling her arse, saying:

– S'posing yer father comes 'ome dinnertime.

He never did. He'd never had a dinner break his whole life. Me and Maxine said nothing to each other, she wasn't scared of Mrs Chambers. She treated her just like a charwoman, sitting there taking it all in with a smile, lighting up a Chesterfield and putting it in an amber holder. Yeah, the real, authentic Lady Muck. I'm not sure I liked her for it, either. None of us were coming out of this with any dignity and I couldn't see what Maxine was doing beyond humiliating us all. I didn't need her to defend my domestic front like she was the Home Guard, the volunteer force. I didn't want her sitting there forcing the comparison because, I had to admit, the old bag's life was humiliating enough. She suffered like Maxine would never suffer.

I'd always seen her life as if she lived it packed in walls of ice, only sometimes she appeared to me elsewhere, in the open. Like now, sipping on her fag but blowing out the tears. Silently bullied by Maxine. I pitied her, shrinking horrified from this feeling, confusing it with longing for family love, as if Maxine was only the mum I never had. That's why I didn't want her there. I didn't want to be seventeen to her thirty-four, but she couldn't see it. She was spellbound by the claustrophobia of our birthright, the stiffling gag of furniture polish and mothballs and Brillo and haughty minisculeness. I couldn't look at Maxine. Instead, I forced myself to look at the old bag, just fascinated by the fact that she was my mother in this room. I'd even started to see her face on the end of my prick when I was having a piss, or about to screw with Maxine, and my theory was that all boys who love older women see their mother's face like that. Then there were other times I saw her when she wasn't there...

I didn't want Maxine to make her hate herself more than she probably did. I didn't want to have to hear one of her 'outbursts,' her 'abdabs,' while Maxine was in earshot. These outbursts, they were manifestations to plug the chasms down no. 51. Like a cow after its calf's been sent to the abbatoir for slaughter. They began with the banging of saucepans and ended with howls at God. The old man would just sit there in the front room unmoved, shuffling through the *TV Times*. In the kitchen an operetta'd be taking place at bursting point, a screaming temperetta with the lid just on, boiling away the sprouts of her life into soggy mush. She combined scraps of prayer with Light Programme rat-pack favourites. Perry Como,

Old Blue Eyes, Tony Bennett:
  The very thought of youuuuuuuuuuuuuuuuuuuuuuuuuuuuuu
  Just makes me want to spewwwwwwwwwwwww
  Oh God in heavennnnnnnnnn
  I hate your sodding guts – ohhh sixes
  And sevennnnnnn…
  – Where are your children? The baggot suddenly said to Maxine.
  – At the seaside with nanny, having a wonderful time, Maxine said, as if she was reading Virginia Woolf out loud. The baggot didn't know what hit her.
  – You should be s'lucky!
  – Yes, aren't I, Mrs Chambers.
  Pinky was locked in the shed for snarling. Maxine even got the baggot to smoke another Chesterfield. She hadn't smoked one of them since the war. Huh, the old man was merchant navy, got torpedoed with a cargo of Chesterfields for the troops. I loved poetic justice normally, but this was leaving me diseased. Then Maxine started giving me those looks. It was exciting her, this stand-off with the char lady and her nubile son.
  – You 'aven't bin to Hawkhurst before then, the baggot said.
  – No, Mrs Chambers, Maxine said. What have I been missing?
  – Nothing, I said.
  Ever after, she was what was missing from the place. For me, Hawkhurst was before and after Maxine. Everything was. Coffee, cigarettes, literature, cars, knowledge of good and evil. It was as if I'd been born between Maxine's legs after all. What a hypocrite she was making of me too, with her wine cellars and avocado pears, that deep husky voice and all her money. I knew about stratification. Snobs and ploggers, Hawkhurst was. Maxine was even a cut above the snobs. She was club casino, that day. Beach and open top. Landed ancestors. What a mess.
  We climbed upstairs after all those looks nearly went down my trousers. They were as visible as her hand. With my old woman just sitting there with the smoking stub of her Chesterfield and a second cup of tea in the front room like she was in the condemned cell. She didn't even have the Jimmy Young show on. You could hear the clock ticking from my bedroom, you could hear the old woman humming to herself as Maxine took her clothes off and knelt on

all fours on my bed, staring at the bare yellow wall. I obeyed. We didn't close the curtains and the sun shone up her arse. She didn't like kissing that day, not in love with me like at Melissa's. Maybe it was Hawkhurst, me, my fucking house and mother, I don't know. It was clinical anyway, scary, completely dislocated. She'd already had her come downstairs. Kiss my back when you come, she said. Kiss my arse, she really meant.

The old woman was banging cupboards downstairs to staunch the coaching springs, or the crying shame. Me and Maxine shared the cigarette. There were goose pimples on her legs. She pulled her clothes on and said:

– Let's walk round the village now. That should be fun.

She went out to the car to fetch a see-through blouse. She didn't like me being upset and saying jealous things. It meant she was going wild again and I was worried by that. Everyone would see her tits, anyway.

– Darling, she said as we walked up Kilner Road.

That Wayne kid nearly fell of his Motabecane when the sun flashed on Maxine's yokes.

– Darling, I put this blouse on for a good reason. I have to take this prescription to the chemist's. You will help me, darling? Say yes, say you love me.

I did all that. I'd already sworn to die for her twice.

It was a Thursday morning. A handful of people, but that was enough. Whistles from builders in a Mini van. Micky Moon and his brother called me Hot Pants Henry. They said I looked like I needed the night off. Stuff like that. Maxine loved it, lapped it up. She wore expensive shades and a scarf made into a bandana, across the forehead and down under the hair at the back of her head. She held my hand and swung my arm as we walked along The Colonnade saying:

– This is lovely. God, I hate London sometimes.

The chemist's had just been taken over by a young couple after Jack retired. He'd been here since before the war, tall, white-haired jolly man who did the magic shows at kids' parties. Nice bell still tinkled over the door, old blue glass jars and bottles on the shelves. The new man didn't wear his white coat, just a baggy check suit. He looked like a German shrink with his round specs and long face, floor mops above both ears and a big shiney forehead, creases like a second mouth. Maxine flipped the shades up and flashed her prescription. I could see she'd forged it. That's what the blouse was for, keep the apothecary from taking too close a look. Poor bloke was a rabbit caught in headlamps. My job was to spot where the jars came from, take a note of anything else helpful. Then I had to go back that night, break in and pinch the valium and sleeping pills. All matter of fact, all explained to me like the instructions on an Airfix kit. My reward would be a whole night in her bed when I could do anything I liked.

Next, we went into Mr Miles's junk shop. She wanted to buy me something, a hip flask of oval glass, leather case and silver flip top. In the off license she bought a quarter bottle of brandy and poured it into the hip flask.

– Tonight, she said, take two swigs before you set off for the chemist's. Don't take the flask with you in case you get tempted and drop it on the job. And no pills, darling. We don't want any more upheavals. Sorry. Just two swigs, sweetheart. Think of me, it'll give you courage.

She took me to the Chinese restaurant next. I'd never been in a restaurant before. Just a willow pattern of sweet and sour pork and lychees in a teacup, but it made me idolize Maxine again beyond all sense of reality. It was only the village Chinky, no big chic for her, specially since everyone in the village was saying inspectors found two dead alsations in Wong's freezer. We were out of control now, it was all wing and prayer. I was too in awe of her sophistication. I mean, for chrissake, I'd never even drunk Kona coffee before. Our house was a Maxwell House, the rest was powder from vending machines. She paid with a cheque, which blew my mind.

Maxine saw no problem with a burglary. She'd hired me, her amateur cracksman. Half in advance, the rest on delivery. If I loved her, I'd have to prove it. If I deserved her, I'd have to do it. She just drove off and left me to it, half-way through the afternoon.

thirteen

At about four o'clock the old woman lit up, fagged out on the sofa with her No 6, a cup of tea and *Womens Realm*. She'd scrubbed the house inside out, expunging all trace of Maxine. She had a face on her that said: you bedder wash your willy before yer father gets 'ome! My guts were still on tumble-dry from the flavour-enhanced sweet-and-sour dog. I said, in a squeaky voice, that I might be going to see a college friend. Casually, adding: probably stay over, take the sleeping bag.

It was easier dealing with her than the old man, but she was the more suspicious. She'd never trusted me, anyway. I was about to break routine on the night of a crime. Come tomorrow, they wouldn't need their clairvoyance. She asked a string of neurotic questions, as if she understood Maxine's visit had upset the apple-cart this time for real. The old man would've just said no you ain't, son, you're stopping right here. She said: and where might that be all of a sudden? I said Benenden. Who with? she said. Bill, I said. Bill who? You know, Bill. Arsenal let him have the week off... And so on. They'd heard it all before. They called it *that Sidney Catt business*.

Sidney Catt, he always managed to materialize when I was out of my depth. The little turd burgler had even been up the village just as me and Maxine were going in the chemist's. This green van, slowing down, pulling up outside that cottage next to the International Stores. SIDNEY CATT ELECTRICIAN TV REPAIRS ANYTHING ELECTRIC UNDERTAKEN. Home-made lettering in white gloss. So there he was, just for the occasion. I knew that handwriting so well. And that tumbling in my guts, just as it had been with Sidney. He'd taught me more about sex and crime than Maxine ever would.

I'd sat next to Sid in class, 1A to 4A. In that capacity I saw him through the upheavals of his first bone, even suffering his attentions after it. He'd been my mate, but the rebuttals were steadfast till I got mine. Then I'd wanted to submit, just the once, but he was all

78

mouth and trouser and hid behind mockery.

Sidney lived up near Babies Castle, part of the village we never really went to, us Kilndown Roaders. Wellington Cottages. They weren't cottages at all, just more drab council houses with arched passages between them, so damp you had to wear Wellingtons. Because of Sidney and the way he boasted, I always thought Wellington Cottages was a playground in the hills. I hadn't even seen him since leaving school, didn't know if he still lived there till I saw it scrawled on his van. They were poor houses with metal framed windows, rust poking through the peeling paint, blisters on doors. No hedges, no trees, just uncut lawn, a rusty fridge on a pile of coal slack and sand. Sidney's house had pools of oil on the garden slabs, fragments of motorbike soaking in filthy metal bowls of fluid. Sidney's fingernails were always black at school, like his windows and half-drawn curtains

We were in 4a. Jessie left us to get on with our fractions while he visited the staff room. Sidney put a ruler across his trouser lap.

– 'Ere, Chambers, look!

The ruler twitched of its own accord.

– Oi got the bone Chambers, hahahaha. Goo on, touch me knob an' see. Made it in woodwork, hahahaha.

I wanted to, only I blushed and said:

– Ain' done me fractions yet.

– Aw carm orn, Chambers. Oi got the 'orn. Wha's wrong wiv yer? Where's all the sex gorn outya?

In Metalwork, Sidney said:

– 'Ere, come t'the bogs. Summing to show yer.

We stood each end of the urinals pretending to slash. My throat choked up, both eyes bulging sideways at Sidney, willing my knob to twitch.

– Guess what oi'm doin, Sidney said.

– Slashin', I said.

– Nah, yer tosspot, haha. Look then, 'Enry. Oi'm avin' a sherman.

Sidney shuffled his fingers over his bone. I was out of my pocket now. Sidney's was white and stiff, a tiny little spike. He started walking backwards towards me, gargling like a ghost. Archer and Marchant were coming along, probably with the same idea, and I could hardly stuff my bender back in its pants. It was pronging about but I still ran back to my metalwork bench where I'd struggled three terms already making a wonky paint scraper for Fritz. Sidney crept up behind me and stamped so hard on my foot I should've hit him.

– Yer fuckin' cory, Pisspot. It were oany me friggin' finger.

And he held up his bone and wiggled it under my nose.

– Haha, seen yawn, though. Boneo, boneo!

Sid was an ugly little runt. Under- nourished, looked like half of one of my silly uncles. Slicked back hair with a cowlick, so everyone called him Tufty. But I still dreamed of fellatio with Sidney's little unit, even ten minutes after screwing Maxine.

After Sid's levitation of his ruler, he became like a little farm terrier rubbing up chair legs. He dragged me off chasing birds from the bus station bogs to the girls' school cemetery. He became a byword in our house for any trouble I might or might not be in. It's that Sidney Catt again, ain' it, boy! If I denied it I got swiped. I had to come up with more and more proposterous lies just to get out the house. That afternoon, the old woman looked at me like that again. If she'd blamed it on him this time I'd've said yes. My life with Sidney Catt was nothing but crime and sex and cheating at maths.

I bagged a bottle of squash and some Garibaldi biscuits. I nicked a slice of stale farmhouse and a lump of cheddar. I can't imagine she didn't guess.

– You're going to that woman, she said. I know it, boy.

I said I was hitching to Benenden, for chrissake. By now she was ringing her hands and biting her knuckles. In this state she'd have been happier if I'd said oh stop moaning, I'm blagging the chemist shop tonight. The false ring of my words were round her eyes as if I'd smacked them one. I felt them burning the back of my head all the way up the road, Sidney urging me on, as if he was there up at the Two Trees waiting for me, just like old times. It was going to turn bad. I knew it then. And I couldn't stop myself. Hurtling into the biggest fucking mess I'd ever been in was the only way out the other side of this Maxine business. Something had to happen, didn't it? I couldn't go on the way things were.

Sid's bone had gone to his head too and he'd started acting hard, dragging me out crumpet-hunting on wet winter evenings round the village. One afternoon we were loitering at the Band Box waiting

80

for the Mary Sheaffe Girls School coaches to come in.

– Fulla birds, Sid Catt said, poking me in the ribs. Sh'll oi git us a couple fer Friday moosh?

I knew it was impossible, but said go on, then. Sid Catt couldn't swim but he had leopardskin trunks. Nor could he whack a football through the woodwork hut window like me. But he smoked, had slit eyes, greasy hair, a Parka with smelly rabbit fur on it, and he could run and answer back at birds. He just wasn't liked much. The hards never let him in their gangs so he was a loner, really, and picked his friends from off the edges and his victims – like me – from the shallow end for non-swimmers. When he left school I thought he'd joined the army, like he said he would. Well, my old man wouldn't let him come try and fix our old tellies. They always blew up after a month. Old black and white stinkers which had pictures like an aquarium full of dishwater. Grey faces swimming in the milk.

So there we were, waiting for the girls:

– 'Ere! Spasticola. Gelz coach in. Jump up an' bang on the back winda when it stops.

I chucked my dufflebag at him, so Sid did the jumping and banging. Ball-bearings fell out of his pocket and he chased them downhill before they found a drain. Two birds hung their mouths out the coach window.

– Naaah-naaah that'll learn yer, squirt! Lostya balls in St Pauls!

Sid pronged 'em with a V-sign.

– You'll be lucky, the other bird said.

Sid Catt pointed at the one who'd called him squirt.

– Whass'er name? Goldfish, or summit?

– Finkya hilarious, doancha. Doan know much, do yer. Anyone knows 'er name's Annette.

I was on my knees, tweaking a ball-bearing from the gutter. I looked up and fancied Annette. Decided I'd do anything to see her again, even go through with Sid's latest jaunt.

– Nah it aint, Annette said. Shurrup yer git, doan tell 'im. Whass yawn then, Gorballs?

The coach started to shudder forward. It was my last chance to be noticed by Annette, so I stood up and squeaked really loud:

– Don't look at 'im: 'e's a flea-bag. 'Is name's Sid Catt.

They cackled at me, all future slags:

81

– Ay? Whassat? Cat what? Cat gotya tongue?

Annette said:

– Dead cat? Oosa dead cat? Whassat make you then, 'is mouse? 'Ere, you two, cat'n mouse! 'Er name's Julie Moon. She goes to Cranbrook Yoof Club Fridiz wiv me...

Every day that week Sid Catt mentioned something new he'd do to Julie.

– Bedder git s'm jonniz 'an we moosh?

Everyday he sang that song to the Chipetos advert:

Jonniz jonniz jonniz
buy a li'l packit fer me
jonniz jonniz jonniz
'alf a crown fer threeeee
'aven 'ad a shag sinz lunchtime
an' now it's 'alf pass freeee
oh jonniz jonniz jonniz...

– Come on, Spasticus, sing along simple!

Sid Catt said he'd nicked the jonniz from Wally Nuns the barbers.

– Two fer me, one fer Spazman. Ain' gonna wear that anorak, are yer, Spazzo?

I told the baggots we were going to see *A Hundred and One Dalmations* at Cranbrook flea-pit. The old man said he'd skin me hide if I weren't back on that ten o'clock bus. Up Hawkhurst bus station Sid Catt gave me a fag to smoke, and started digging a Fruit & Nut out the chocolate machine with his penknife. I sucked on the filter end of my Numbey and Sid Catt stamped on my foot.

– You said yer smoked, yer fuckin' pikey! Dressed like a fuckin' pikey an' all.

Sid Catt was in his beige flares, winkle-pickers, fake suede safari jacket, white rollneck pullover. This was a bad omen. My own brown terylenes had infinitesimal flares which hung too high over my shoes like the vicar's. My daring Carnaby Street look was the red rollneck under a pink nylon shirt.

One sniff at Cranbrook Youth Club and my future went numb. It was a right shop for a smacking. In the lobby Sid Catt tried to bluster it out, but after a minute was reduced to shuffling his winkle-pickers in the corner. He still pretended to be a regular, polishing his points up the back of his trousers, saying he was fuckin' ready for it, ain't chew? Cupped his Numbeys like a skinhead when some real yobs scuffed in, gobs like cement mixers going on the Juicy Fruit, more *Brut* than fart, as it was early. Sid Catt was looking everywhere for Julie Moon, even up on the ceiling. Shoved aside in the dance-floor doorway by this chacking hard in a Crombie and two-tones:

– Art the fackin' wye, cunt.

And Sid Catt going:

– Sorry-sorry-sorry mate.

One look at that dance-floor turned my guts to Marmite. It was phonebox-red, cunt-red, it was the inside of a cunny like a tardis. I saw hardnuts back-to-front on plastic chairs or stomping shincrackers in time with Long Shot Kickee Bucket and Skin'ead Moonstomp. This bird in a yellow mini-skirt screamed as she got dragged into a dark corner when they played Wet Dream. Sid Catt was making them in-out-in-out dirty noises: uh-uh-uh-uh. He said he could smell that bird getting it from here, right up her breakfast. I needed to get a fist round my Pope and give it a pasting. Sid Catt said them Annettes and Julies were just slags keeping us waiting and waiting. I reckoned we'd been tricked.

– They was on the Sandhurst coach, spunk-'ead, I said.

– Oi shittin'-well know that, Spazzo.

But I could see he hadn't thought of that. In the phonebox I looked up MOON in the directory and dialled Mrs Moon with my penny. She was at Sandhurst Youth Club, not Cranbrook, Julie Drooly was.

By 8.15 we were running back out of Hawkhurst Bus Station in the opposite direction along the Sandhurst Road. I got the stitch and had to lean, the sound of winkle-pickers was swallowed up in the dark. The old man could come along any minute. I spewed my chips up over the fence. As long as Annette was there... I'd get a thrashing anyway, there was no way out of this. The signpost said Sandhurst 1. Henry 0.

Sandhurst Youth Club was in the church hall back of the village green, quiet and sleepy and the smell of Sunday School, dark green wooden door, boys and girls in my sort of Friday best. Cordaroys ironed the wrong way into cricket pads, nice frocks or a flowered blouse. They sat on brown canvas chairs, feet up on wooden chests full of Hymnals and Girl Guides' regalia. Little boys played ping-pong. I hung back in the porch and washed my sicky mouth out with water from a brass tap with the flower rota pinned nearby. I wiped a bit of sick off my shoe on the big black-out drapes. Sid Catt had the cards out showing off a trick. Two four-eyed squirts played draughts on a collapsible picnic table. The big Smith clock said ten to nine.

I'd got to heaven and could only stay half an hour. I was so excited that there were no skinheads and borstal boys, I went straight in and blurted:

– Where's Annette then, Sid?

I'd just started to rub my hands together when I saw her, sitting on the rockabilly knee of the pikey she loved. He was rocking her up and down in time with the record player, singing together:

Two lickle boys 'ad two lickle toys...

– Awww, put *Albatross* on an' turn the lights out.

Then Archer and Marchant from class walked in, smelling of a fag each. Annette's brother said:

– Caw, fuck me, it's Pisspot and Catshit. Fort you two was goin' darn Cranbrook.

Annette leaned back in the pikey's arms. *Albatross* thrashed inside the little rabbit hutch of a record player. Sid Catt said:

– Pisspot's after your sister.

– Year, I said , 'n yaw after July Drooly wiv a pockit fulla rubbers, Catshit.

I got some hair yanked out and a big tweak on the tit for that. Julie Drooly was up in the attic getting her ackers fumbled so we played ping-pong doubles. The ball spun under pikey's chair first ralley.

– Goo gid it, Pisspot, yer useless spanner. You missed it.

The pikey was Reggie Rummery. He didn't have all night, he was on probation. White hipsters, leather jerkin. I stood before his throne.

– Lostya balls, China?

When I dogged under the chair to pick it up I felt his winkle-picker rest on my back.

– Shoe shine! Shoe shine! Hahaha.

Annette was laughing too, but Sid Catt howled most:

– Shit eemself at Cranbrook, din 'e. Ain' takin' 'im no more wivvout eez nappies.

Reggie screwed Sid Catt out:

84

– Oi, laughin' policeman. Shut your cake'ole an' change the record.

Albatross was finished, Sid Catt put on *Young Girl*. Annette sang along: *You should be home wiv your muvver, you're jussa baby in disguise ...*

Reggie said:

– Say please.

I said please. Annette said:

– Poor Buster.

It was only five past ten when Buster opened the front gate but they fell on me like guard dogs. The bag knew. *Hundred and One Dalmations* her blinkin' foot! Phoned Sid Catt's dad, Kit. Kit Catt.

– Stop yer bloomin' smirk, lad.

They'd phoned the police, reported me missing, possible runaway, up to no good. Harold Wilson was on the News too, so the old man was in no mood for fibs.

– Bloody Labour knockers. Knock-knock bloody knock.

The old bag was checking the timetables.

– What the flippin' Jesus you bin up to, boy?

I walked three miles towards Benenden, looking for a camp. I stashed down behind some stooks in a field high above the lane, hidden by a spinney. I read *Undertones of War* for three hours propped on camping elbows, an infantryman at rest before the final push. No haymaker at simple supper from some poncey Millais painting. The Pre-Raphaelites were dead. I was a real war poet now. I had a sweetheart far away that I might never see again.

About half-eight I got in the sleeping bag, finished off the Garibaldis, and kipped. I woke at midnight and thought no, I couldn't do it after all. Go back to sleep. But I'd promised, I loved her, she was counting on me, and I'd failed her once already. I started the long skice back to the village down the middle of the road. It was warm, I could hardly see my feet. I was enjoying this bit too, drifting in the dark, half-wilting from fatigue. The other half of me strummed with fear and excitement. I put my fingers down my trousers and sniffed Maxine on the end of them. It pushed me on, route marching now, life and death, the same road I'd run down with Sid Catt. Oh fuck. I was alongside the copse at the top of Kilner Road and I could feel that hole in the ground where the big house had been. It was so dead I decided to just walk straight through the village. It was easier than climbing over the backs of a hundred walls, or whatever there was behind the houses leading up to The Colonnade. That way I'd not be alerting a potential two dozen people while steeplechasing to the chemist's. Not a single car had passed me in three miles. The traffic lights were green facing me, the streetlamps were out, the shops were dark. I walked past the front of the chemist's and turned right down Cranbrook Road. The only people who could see me would live above the Draper's. Macey, a greaser who rode a three-wheeler chopper lived there. I was suprised he hadn't busted the place himself.

I was looking for the back door. I took the cinders track by the estate agents. This led along the back of The Colonnade. I shinned a freshly creosoted shiplap fence and there I was, stood looking at the burglar's entrance of the chemist's. Two swigs on the hip flask, carried against instructions to the scene of the crime. It really worked. Perhaps it always does the first time. It cleared my head, that is clarified it, like clarified butter. I learned several things about myself. One: that I wasn't a natural burglar. Two: that the only way out of the mess my life was in was to get caught – an interesting option from all points. Things like that change your life for sure. And I wanted change, didn't I?

I was holding my sleeping bag, which I'd meant to stash in Copt Hall field, but that was fine. It would be useful: I needed something to carry off the big jars in, the swag and doss. I undid the ties and half-unrolled it, put my fist inside and tried pushing at the door glass. Hoping, I suppose, that it would just fall out like a piece of paper or something. I pushed harder, it was like a newborn baby's fist in a boxing glove. The rustling seemed so loud I thought Macey would be over soon to help me out. But I pushed on, a bit harder each time. It struck me then that I really didn't know what I was doing. Nor what would happen if the glass broke. I hadn't considered if there might be a burglar alarm. This was Russian roulette. If the alarm went off I'd scoop along the back fences and make for the nearest darkness. But wasn't I clever, bringing the sleeping bag. You lay it on top of fences and belly-flop army style over, like we did as kids.

Then the glass cracked, so unexpectedly I just stood waiting.

Maybe I thought the chemist's would just surrender and open the door itself. Or just throw the pharmaceuticals out for hostages. I couldn't see my way to advancing beyond cracking glass. I was too tired. I could've curled up in that sleeping bag where I stood. I couldn't prise the segments out, I didn't have my crib-cracking tools on me that night. Raffles had them, and he must've leant me Bunny instead. Maxine seemed a long long way off from this, there really was no logical connection. It didn't feel as if she was running operations from her bed. I could imagine Pre-Raphaelite ghosts talking to me in graveyards, but I couldn't muster up an image of Maxine laying there fingering her piss-flaps, thinking of her hero out there in the pretty village night, risking his liberty so she could quench her death-wish. But I could picture my old baggots right then, snapping awake and saying: where's that boy? He's up to malarky.

All success was luck. Like the way Jesus told it to Parson Potter, only Parson Potter left out the luck bit in his sermons. Mine was a fucking great noise just yards away as the yards fly. An articulated stinker of the night grinds up the hill. The light was red. It could've been a gypsum lorry, or a logger or continental freight. Who cared, the roar it had to make when the light changed, just to lip the brow, might've woken all Hawkhurst. But it covered my impulsive battering. Glass down, door open, I was in, no alarm. The sleeping bag was suddenly a drag, like doing a slow dance on a crowded bus. I knocked two stands of boiled throat sweets over. Well, I didn't – but I could've. I wasn't even in the shop, just a backroom with a sink and kettle and stuff. I only had eyes for Maxine's jars. The light was half slant from the traffic lights so I used blind logic… Dr Dispenser was standing there, he reached here, unscrewed that … bullseye. No wonder he had his arm round the jar as if it was a Christmas goose. It had to weigh a ton, and it was only three-quarters full, thousands of blue 25mg Valiums. I was just about to finger it when I checked myself. Finger prints. They might not even realise it was empty, Maxine's prescription gulled him after all. Then I had the brainwave: tip the contents into the doss bag, leave a few in the jar. You never know. Old Jeckel might even put the cracked door down to the wind or a clumsy dustman, specially if I managed to lock it again.

That's what I did. A big bulge of mixed pills and a few small boxes of glass phials. The apple juice was all sold out, or I'd've had a swig for old time's sake. Everything seemed too long ago. I'd just become old.

fourteen

I thought of Mr James, master of equations, a man of acute perception. He'd got it wrong when he'd said I could go to University. I thought of him, because anyone in my shoes would think of those he was about to disappoint. My future flashing out of reach before me as I fell. I wouldn't be going anywhere; I think I knew I'd crossed that point of no return. Mr James hadn't seen the doom in it, that you shouldn't dish out hope to the starving of 4a when Sid Catt was the intellectual mean.

Mr James, a tubular Welsh slag-heap in thornproof trousers with a heart of coal. Headache brows, parade-ground brogues, the only master at Swattenden who commanded and won. His wrath was molten lava. He lived with his housekeeper on the edge of the village in a dark heavy house, up Sid Catt's way and all. The only Welsh-looking slate-roofed tip-toe-past-it house in Hawkhurst. The only Sir in the school who tolerated his nickname, Jessie James.

Like everyone else, I was terrified of upsetting him. He did fractions and algebra. The kinder he was, the more monumental his authority. He told stories of his own dragon days at school, three miles up the coal valley, over the shunting yards. He'd run home every dinnertime with his algebra book to eat his mam-made hot cawl in the green kitchen that mam scrubbed with brimstone every morning. Algebra was his idea of a boy's fun. No blackened footballs under gas lamps for our Jessie. His mam'd said: University for you, boy. And all that running to and fro kept him fit as a sack of leeks. When he went to the great capital of England for his teacher training, he won himself a place in the London Welsh Rugby Football Club.

Jessie said to me:

– You, boy, could go to University if you try hard.

We were standing at the top window, and down in the playground a swarm of grey boys played Man Utd v Benfica.

– Where's University, Sir? Is it far?

– University, thick-head, is a goal only one boy from this school ever kicked before.

He pointed down into Hell, where Archer and Marchant twanged a lazzie band on Lowman's ear'ole, and Eliot wouldn't pass to Keeves who was a useless woman, all knees and new brown boots.

– There is not a BOOOOOYYYYYYYY down there Chambers, he said jabbing his parsnip stub of finger on the glass, who has your BRRRRRRRRAINNNS. Now, run along and think about Univerrrrsity.

I ran along, straight into Sidney Catt who coerced me into telling him what Jessie had wanted.

– Cor, fuck me, pull the other one, Pisspot. You ain' no more brains'n a fish.

The old woman called me Simple Simon and said Jessie had no right to put ideas like that into boys' heads.

When I applied to the West Kent College to do some levels on my step to University, the already disappointed baggots threw up their hands and said well, if I wanted to make a fool of myself that was my funeral. Then Ma baggot suffered humiliation up the tobacconist's over it from Dennis, who was the only one wouldn't be disappointed. He would be thrilled at my escapade. Before he'd pranged his kit-car on a tree down The Lanes, Dennis had long blonde hair, sporty gear, flashy watch, birds on his bonnet outside The Oak. He'd been to the Bunny Club too. Used to be a volunteer fireman and all. After his prang he wore a cloth cap over pudding-basin haircuts and went round with a droopy chin. His old man handed the tobacconists over to him. The baggot went in there once a week.

– Ooz zis stuff for then, Mrs Chambers? You doan smoke a poipe.

– My boy said 'e wants to try one, if you doan mind.

Christ, it came up in an argument, that. They caught me smoking, of smoking age. I said I bet they wouldn't moan if I smoked a pipe up the fuckin' golf club.

– Bit up top, in 'e, your boy? Dennis said.

– Yerse, yer might say that. Quite brainy.

– Nah, that ain' what oi meant! Up top. I mean, yer don't see 'im, you know, lookin' normal, way he dresses. I've sin 'im wiv 'andbags…

– Now look 'ere, you! My boy's brainy, so enough o' your cheek. He's goin' t'Uneeversity, I'll 'ave you know, Mr Clever-Clogs.

Every time he spotted me, he rushed to his shop door and shouted: watchyear professor! On yer way t'university?

I was scared of Maxine for the first time. And scared of what she'd've done if I'd said no. IrratBiotional, because the reason she wanted me to blag the chemist's was now obvious, and I'd somehow put it aside, thinking that whatever happened I'd at least have my night with her first. She wanted to kill herself some other way. She'd said she was bored cutting her arms. Naïvely, I thought she meant all that was over now she'd found me. But probably not. This was more exciting for her, laying in bed, thinking of me dispensing her way out. My reward as good as necrophilia, shinning up the Hospice drainpipe into her room.

It was 3am by the time I was leafing through the trees at Copt Hall looking for a hide-out. By then I knew I should've planned it better. Maxine wanted me to get the first bus out to Tunbridge Wells. She'd be waiting, we were going to have a naked breakfast. She'd let me lay on top of her and kiss her on the lips. Lying in state, she'd be. She'd survived at least two severed main arteries. They gave her three pints of blood for soaking the back page of *The New Statesman*. Which meant that when I'd left her that time, she was already nearly half-dead. I don't know, I just didn't know. I had to get these pills to Tunbridge Wells, that's all. I had to be with her. She'd given me the bus fare, anyway. My sacrifice was turning into sour exhaustion, and fear stepped in at last and went right through me. I was so cold.

It would've been too suspicious if I emerged from the woods like a tramp with a sack. I was at the top of my own road again, right outside the bus station. All roads to life started there. I'd be getting the 7.30, probably about the time the break-in would be discovered. Fatty Stamp gladly making a citizen's arrest with his ticket machine. Halfway to Tunbridge Wells, like Crippen on the Queen Mary.

It would be light in an hour or two. I was the wrong side of the village to start hitching to Tunbridge Wells. I couldn't risk the walk back through the village either. I had to bushwack a detour under cover. Down Little Switzerland, up Talbot Road, down the "Lawns" and out onto the Flimwell Road. It would take an hour or more.

The pills were rattling loose in the sleeping bag. Any self-righteous phantasy about being the village poacher gave way to the universal comdemnation coming to me. I was a common burglar. It was a drug crime. It dawned on me that I'd just ruined my life for good. Or the half of it Maxine hadn't already ruined. But her ruin was designed, a Gothic ruin. A folly. Mine was a fatal accident, a jerry-built low-rise collapsed in a heap of poor materials. I just wished I'd kipped, woken up, stashed the bag. Then I'd've hung about, sort of arrived home for breakfast as if I'd done a night shift. If I'd got something to put the pills in, I could've caught the bus mid-morning, clean and fresh. The poor old village sergeant standing on The Colonnade scratching his big top. London gang musta dunnit.

It was still dark when I poked my face out onto the Flimwell Road. Where the public footpath skirts Theobalds, snobstown two-up two-downs, opposite Oakfield, just up from Parson Potter's Manse. I heard a milk float, then a lorry. A car came into the village, so I stepped from view. Everything seemed so innocent and normal as it passed. Another dawn about to crack open like a fresh farm egg. The birds struck up their chorus one by one. Another hot day when people just lazed about, slowly and happily like bot flies on cowclats. A second car was coming, up the Flimwell Road this time, headlights full. Oh, what the fuck, I thought, and stepped out, thumb up. Probably a builder on his way to work. My old schoolmates in a Mini Van. They recognised me, yes, the car stopped. The thing with hitching is you never looked at the car till it stopped. Like you don't care, like you're not desperate.

– Where you off to, mate? the copper said, flinging the door open.

Talk about lucid. I knew this footpath blindfold and flew down it thinking I had to ditch the pills first. The best way to do that was dump them in the pond back of Marlborough House Prep-school. Help the sticklebacks cope with having to live with spikes and prep-school kids. The copper made a mistake. He hesitated, got his torch out the car, then tried running into blindness with the beam on. I had two hundred yards on him. He wouldn't know about the pond. The trouble was it sat in the open and there wasn't time. I had to come up with another idea as I ran, so I carried on down the footpath, all the way to where this ditch of a stream runs under a little bridge. I unrolled the sack, tipped it upside down. All the pills plinked in a shower and carried away on a swift little flash of current under the trees. I even had time to roll the sleeping bag up and stuff it in the holly hedge.

The sun was about to rise. I was walking back up the track when I came face-to-face with the copper. I had my story all worked out. He wasn't afraid of me, that was a good sign. He even smiled.

– Henry Chambers? he said. Are you Henry Chambers?

– Yes, I said. Then I realised. How the fuck did he know that?

– We've been looking for you. This yours?

He was holding out a book, *Undertones Of War*, my name written in the front.

– Where'd you find that?

– Where d'yer think! Makes no difference. You were seen and heard by half the Colonnade. Yer mum's in a bad way. Really upset her, you 'ave.

fifteen

Maxine said we could meet one more time. Summer had gone, it was wet under the trees, out with the first mist, down with the apples, mould and maggots rolling in the dead leaves, wasps dying like curled-up cellophane. A half-moon rose in the afternoon, and you noticed the swallows had gone. Your hands shrivelled up, your tea went cold before you'd got the cap back on the thermos. Butterflies just hit the ground beside you, wings of rag, too exhausted to get up. Back-end of September, a week before my case came up at the Magistrate's Court. I'd stand where O so many Swattenden boys had stood before me. We'd answered to a long list of crimes, like car theft, vandalism, assault, GBH, possession, eel poaching, receiving stolen property, drunken driving. I was the first to blag a chemists'.

That morning I waited up the High Street, bold as brass, they said. Look? They looked all right, especially that early in the morning. Wondering whose window I'd just broke, whose drainpipe I'd shinned down. I waited as the sun rose like spilt milk in a lemon sky. The clock on Dunks Almhouses still stuck on last wintertime. The sun was barely above ground, the wormcast lawns were spored in dew and sagging webs. The spire of All Saints began to yellow.

The maroon Austin Maxine. Her hair was tied back, the sunglasses cut us off. She wound the window down, chucked a fag-end out, touched my face. Her black dress with red roses big as cabbages. I lit two fags and passed her one. She squeezed my hand as if we were in for a rough ride, and away we went.

She didn't know anything, only that something had gone wrong. When I hadn't appeared with the pills, she'd rung. The ratbag had answered and Maxine got what for. The evil woman speech, the leave my boy alone plea. The go back to your bloody husband shit. The shame she'd brought on them all. Maxine guessed I'd been caught. And she knew I wouldn't give her away. I didn't, and I should've.

– Lucky for you, I said. Mum fuckin' died, didn't she. Shame

94

and a massive heart attack.

O my Angel of Death. She kept that car straight as a die when I told her this. She didn't twitch a wing muscle, drop a flower, snap a stem. Death was just her business.

– So ashamed, I said. She took my secret to the grave. She never told my old man about you. Can you believe it?

I said the shame was probably me being charged. It was in the paper. *Local Youth Charged in Chemist Shop Break-In*. Instead of *Local Boy goes to University* ... She was throwing up all week, panic attacks, under sedation, agraphobic. No mother's heart can take that.

It wasn't true, of course. She hadn't really died, except by slow degrees and a lot faster than before. I told Maxine this because she'd sacrificed me. I needed to make her face some of her culpability. I wanted it to link us so she'd rescue me, finally. She'd suffered no shame whatsoever. In fact, she basked in the medical attention, and they wrote poems about her. Those Chelsea poets in their Chelsea scarves. Their language was as ignoble as a skinhead's. As for Hawkhurst, she couldn't imagine what it was like now, nor did she try. Dennis jumping out the tobacconists to call me Burglar Bill every day. I thought he was funny, actually. He said I was so fucking stupid because I'd got the wrong shop. I'd obviously meant to do his tobacconist's, next door. He'd even left my favourite fags, Raffles, out on the counter for me. I wished I had done him. Damn sight more useful. Even to Maxine, never seen without a Chesterfield. No-one called me Raffles, though, and Maxine said: Poor Pisspot. That was fuckin' all. I could tell the judge about her.

– Is that what you want? she said.

We drove a long way, into East Kent.

– Where we going? I said.

– To my home, she said.

Didn't she mean: to my long home? You know who said that, Jane Eyre's friend dying of fever at that school. She had so many homes, Maxine. Every letter came from somewhere else. Were we going to live in one together, then?

– No, she said. I wish we could...

She was taking me to the house where she was born. The big treat. It was even like a Sunday drive, the empty lanes, the silent farms where the warm eggs were just collected, the stirring of the elms in an eight o' clock breeze. Maxine drove in bare feet. On a long straight stretch of road, she leaned over and kissed me on the lips, letting the car drive itself. Long home after all then? A death kiss if ever there was one, the car beginning to veer into the oncoming lane as she lingered on me. I refused to flinch. I was almost pursuaded that we should die together in the crash, and if we survived we'd be inseparable, life or death she'd be mine, Gerald would know all about it from the police...

We came to a fork in the road. *Strictly Private*, poplars along a stream, meadows daubed in hare's-foot and rose bay. This was the big house at last, the parting gift. A glimpse of what I couldn't have. The final lesson, the last exam. The uninhabitable mansions of my mind. We were in Hardfarthing Park. Seat of the dishonorable Maxine Pollenfex. Source of the one true void. From there it dripped and trickled till finally, as a gushing stream, it flowed into Hawkhurst, sweet water of infection.

The left pier of an entrance gate, a stone lion with its paw on a bowl of fruit. The great and mighty Pollenfexes conquer the banana-backed boys, the little grapes who cling to the walls. The windows were all thrown open, a yellow duster appeared in one. Flip-flap. We left the car doors open and stood on the gravel, looking. Me at the house, the hall, the fuckin' mansion ... whatever. And Maxine was looking at me. This was all about inpenetrable gulf, not generation gap, not even class difference. This was chasm-size, this was the abyss. This was that missing link in my education, Maxine saying: see, my world really is uninhabitable, even by us. It's dead, it's deadly. It's doomed. It's a ruin. Stay away, save yourself. Your mum was right.

We walked through the front doors, and circled room by oak-panelled room. All the furniture was embalmed under anti-macassars. Maxine said her parents still lived there, but they were in Italy while the wood treatment people were in, prior to it going on the market. One day it would be a luxury hotel. The upper class was over. They were selling up and going abroad. The valets and the maids and the likes of us trampled in, mop, bucket and vacuum cleaner.

Behind the house – I nearly said round the back, as if there'd be dustbins and a coal bunker – was an Italian garden. Arched gate, dove-cote. There were fountains, goldfish pools, statuettes, lovers' walk, aboretum. A ha-ha just like I'd read about for A Level in *Mansfield Park,* looking down through the meadow to a leg-of-mutton lake, lily-pads and swans. She took the last drag on a Chesterfield and said: watch this. She threw the dog-end into a pool and the goldfish took it in turns to suck on it.

– They all smoke, she said, but the joke fell flat. We did the jokes in the working class, Maxine. And I knew more about fish than you.

We drove another mile, to a village still in the park. The churchyard where the family were buried. There were half a dozen Maxine Pollenfexes, aged 2-52. All the Pollenfexes, their babies, their bastards, their lovers, their dogs and their lovers' fuckin' poems, probably. She unlocked the door of the small cottage opposite. Here were the avocados, the cheese, the wine. She made coffee and we ate toast. It wasn't nine o'clock yet.

– This was nanny's cottage, she said.

– Oh, I see.

– Do you? Will you ever understand us?

Who did she mean? Me and her? Or "them?"

She showed me her room.

– I lived here till the day I was married.

This was like my own bedroom. A tiny cold room with blue striped wallpaper and childs' drawings pinned to the wall. Those Freida Khalo faces, the girl Maxine crying and bleeding or walking into the open doors of the tombs opposite. I looked out the window, smack onto a gravestone with the words: A TRUE LOVE GONE TO THEE — Maxine Pollenfex, age forty-five. She must've woken up every morning, looked out the window and thought: I've thirty-five years left, thirty-four years left, thirty-three years…

There was a trunk on the floor and a pile of crumpled paper. All her own keepsakes and more cut-throats. And her wedding photograph, in the rubbish bin. I picked it out and made her write on it: *To my Darling Henry.* It was signed by Swaebe of Mayfair, and this was the one they stuck in *Country Life.* A black and white photo of a nineteen-year-old stunner tilting her head. Big dark eyes lowered, a swept-up piled shell of deep auburn hair, Roman nose, lips like crescents of tangerine. Her wedding dress is a bell jar, all hoops and farthingales and a runaway train that plunges off the border. She holds a spray of flowers, supplicates them. They sit on a transparent base as if they're part of the dress, like a whole field heaped in arms covered by long, loose silk gloves. Beside her, there's a gilt ornate table where more flowers tumble: lillies, daffodils, carnations. And, bigger than a doorway, hang the family portraits.

I sobbed my heart out then. Darling, she said, don't spoil it. We were near the end now, she was on her deathbed. She undressed, I took up my place, did what she asked and let her dig this spike of green glass into her wrist. Just let me fucking die, she said.

PART TWO

seventeen

I'd only seen one dead body, myself. On the way to college one morning on the 88, the double-decker. It was winter, ice and sun, the other side of Flimwell where the dual carriageway reverted to single lane. A lorry driver blinded by the sun swerved to avoid a cyclist, hit the ice rink, smack-on with a white mini-van with four builders inside. One of them was Mr Soar from down our road. I used to see him walking past every morning in his donkey jacket, fag behind his ear, flask poking out the top of his old gas mask bag. The ambulance hadn't arrived yet but old Soar was laying at the side of the road on his back, still in his donkey jacket. Must've already smoked the fag. His eyes were wide open, a short trickle of blood running from his mouth. Me and the bus driver stood looking at him, and the bus driver said: he's a gonner. I kept thinking about that: a gonner. A gonner. Going, gone, gonner. The blokes in the Mini were all groaning and saying help, oooh my legs, get us out, but they were all crushed in. I rolled them fags and passed them through the window. Then lit them all up. When the Police came they said I could've blown everyone to fucking kingdom come. But the blokes in the van knew me after that, always give us a nod up the village.

I thought Maxine was a gonner till the letter came. She was supposed to be. I'd already begun her obituary. But it was a trick, her dramatic twist. She could cut an artery as matter-of-factly as most of us pick our bogies.

Darling Henry
  I do not wish to write this. I pray you will understand and try not to be bitter about me. Coming back here was worse than I expected. I do not propose to bore and entangle you with the sordid details of my marriage. For the sake of my children (whom Gerald is intending to take away from me on the grounds of mental instability) I desperately wish to keep a family unit together. Also, whatever has gone between

101

me and Gerald, I still hold great affection for him. We have lived together for over ten years. I am afraid your presence in my life, no matter how welcome, is merely an added complication. Also, a dangerous one for us both.

Henry, have faith in yourself. You have so much to offer, and so much that you could achieve. Try not to drown in your emotions – I know this is hard.

Please, darling, at the moment do not ring, write, or attempt to see me again. Good luck, sweetheart, do not even despair over another – none of us are worth it. Perhaps, later, when you feel less hateful towards me, we can write as friends. As always, I will wonder how you are getting on. I was so flattered that you would dedicate a book to me – perhaps one day, having written some melancholy poems of autumn, you still will? A leaf half-remembered, blown to the wind.

I enclose with this the softness of my love.

Maxine

Thank you for everything, thank you – it meant so much and still does. I feel pain too.

My old man said he couldn't bear to show his face at work any more because of me, the crying shame, but it didn't stop him going there at seven o'clock every morning. Chris Kirby over the road had just started work under him. He told me the old man swore worse than anyone there. Called Chris a 'bastard cunt' on his first day. I was amazed at this. I'd never heard him swear, nor had my old woman, I bet. So maybe a bit of shame there wouldn't have gone amiss, the two-faced git, blaming all his life's failure on me now. What right did he have to be so 'flamin' disappointed' in me, as he put it? I'd rather he'd've called me a bastard cunt and got it over with. But he just said:

– Get off yer backside, boy, and find yerself a job o' work like the magistrate told yer to.

When he got all fuckin' het up it sounded like he said 'find yerself a Jabberwok.'

You'd think there hadn't been a scandal in the village since Flick had a bun. She soon disappeared from the village though, after that rumpus down the Baptist Chapel. Organ Morgan stopped Brim Stone from seeing her again. He soon forgot her, anyway. The baby was adopted and Flick married a prison officer in Chatham. All concerned hoped a similar clean-up might be done in my case. The old cunt said I was lucky not to be in jail. The magistrate said I had to repay the debt I owed society. Six months suspended, six months probation, £100 fine. Is that all society was worth?

At first, I did as Maxine asked. I let the cold months come between us and put out the fire. She didn't write that friendly letter in return for my loyal silence. So I finished my long poem to her, which I had to publish. I mean really publish, in *Poetry Review,* so she'd see it and know what she'd done, in the cause of this repayment.

Maxine subscribed to *Poetry Review,* see. She'd been to writing classes with famous poets. She'd had affairs with these poets. She called them Tom and Colin and Dan, making it sound like Henry wouldn't sit right among *Notes on Contributors. Poetry Review* rejected it, one of those multiple choice rejection slips. That wouldn't do. I couldn't repay Maxine on the never-never.

It was only under scrutiny that I wondered who I was, or who I had to be to stop losing. I wasn't a Pre-Raphaelite any more, of course. I was Post-Maxine, and anything I read about, it all seemed good to me. I'd written First World War poetry, a Russian emigré monologue, a Viking lament and a modernist epic on the Thames with Roman names. Made no difference, poetry, in the workaday world. Was the old cunt right? Girls still called me Pisspot, boys called me Chambers. Some of the hards had a grudging respect for me now, after my famous Hawkhurst crime of passion. The Hawks wanted me to play for them again, if I got a haircut or a tattoo and did road-run and started drinking beer up The Cricketers.

I didn't wear the tweed hacking jacket or the green loons, long gone threadbare. The desert boots still fitted and had a few leagues of use in them. I might've walked through Hawkhurst with a silver-topped cane, sometimes. It made the palm of my hand go blue, though. My hair was cotted over my shoulder but the scruff of itchy beard had gone with my début shave. I was trying to look more straight, neutral, so I could flip between the stratas and see where it got me. As winter was coming, I got a clothing voucher from the social which I spent unwisely: woollen flares with a thirty-two-inch bore which dragged in the grit. Grey velvet jacket and a pink shirt. The result was androgeny, Diamond Dogs. I went up the library twice a week, a room not much bigger than a fire engine because it was in the old fire station. I read what was available: science fiction and detective novels.

I talked to no-one. There was no-one to talk to, except this cat I'd got to know on one of my walks. I was reduced to asking it if it remembered me from the day before. It was like The Cheshire Cat, and always grinned if you were getting things right in your life, as if it was an oracle. It was having a shite out of its oracle the first time I saw it, making the parabolic opposite of a grin, screwing up its eyes because even to a cat that vision of myself was so infinitesimal. We didn't have cats, of course – just Pinky, the Ma Aids of the dog world. The old woman hated moggies, blamed anything smelly on a perishin' cat, like Gran did. Our family oracle was the football pools coupon. Pinky never grinned in her whole life, prophetic snarl like a rictus as the Chambers family fulfilled this dog's sense of what was right with the world of no. 51. She was so old now she'd started crapping her own skeleton, bone by bone. The old bastard collected them and showed the vet every bleached fragment from Pinky's poo. The vet said hmmm, that looks like cartilage to me, George. She's breaking up, blown the head gasket…

Maxine had said I should find a nice girl and forget her. Even back in summer, she'd said I should go out with some girl at college, but when I'd mentioned one of them once, Maxine screamed: I HATE HER.

I tried to get a girl for winter, to put Maxine aside, but you couldn't get a crumpet voucher off the dole. I tried to get savvy, as the old man insisted, looking through the job adverts. I also 'ran away' to London twice. Actually, over girls who didn't really want to see me, like Karen from Theydon Bois. I met her in the graveyard up The Moor one Sunday when I was pretending to sketch opposite Lillesden Girls School, boarders 5-18, but really hoping to catch a stray one come in for a fag behind a tomb, like they often did. Karen had a spikey face and a pierced ear with a cross, a touch of patchouli and a shaggy afghan coat with chinks of coloured mirror sewn in. I tried painting her two Sundays in a row. She put up with me because she was a rebel, I gave her fags, her old man was a gangster and I was out of bounds. I was a public school wheeze now, the villain of the colour plates: If you get seen talking to that rotter, Jenny said as Karen stepped from the churchyard, you're sure to be expelled.

Half-term I got her phone number from directory enquiries. Kept ringing it but she didn't want to meet, she'd got a holiday job in Dolcis, Oxford Street. She said the mafia fixed it up for her, thinking it would scare me off. But I sold my birthday presents for extra cash down Mr Miles Hock Box and stalked Oxford Street all morning, catching Karen at dinnertime. I told her all my friends were dead or in prison and she believed me, even seemed to like me a little after that. Once we sat under a tree in Hyde Park and smoked a joint, but she wouldn't let me put my arm round her.

In the afternoon we went to see the Pre-Raphaelite collection at the National Gallery. Even this failed to increase my attraction. She only broke her silence after peering at a dozen paintings. She leaned forward, concentrating on the little brass plate at the foot of the frame on a Holman Hunt and said in a loud voice: hmmm, I really really loike *Bequest*. It wasn't in me to ridicule ignorance, but I never wanted to see her again. I went on to the Rossetti exhibition alone, to renew my membership of the Brotherhood out of disillusionment, guilt, the past. As I stood looking at the *Beata Beatrix,* one of half a dozen copies that DGR painted, I saw, in the light, a hair on the painting. I stepped across the thick security rope and examined it. It was actually stuck into the paint: a hair off Dante Gabriel Rossetti's own head. It had to be. I plucked at it, snapped it out, then pressed it quickly between the pages of my notebook. I had a relic of DGR himself.

I was sleeping on a bench at Charing Cross that night, when the St Mungo's soup run came with bread and oxtail soup. It occured to me that Maxine might come along with the soup; it was the sort of thing these Maxines did. Volunteering to get over an affair with a poet, that is. The benches were uncomfortable and some old tramp told me to kip on the football special in the sidings. I woke up in Ashford and had to fuckin' hitch back to Hawkhurst. When I opened the notebook to add Rossetti's hair to Maxine's shrine, it crumbled to dust.

eighteen

You enter Calverly Park in Tunbridge Wells through the wooden swing gate by the sandstone lodge. The semi-circular private carriageway's bounded one side by tall hedgerows. Behind them, on the shoulders of sloping lawns, stand nineteen different villas built by Decimus Burton. Tall, silent, Italianate, cold damp sandstone and the whites of elongated shutters, bow and canted bays, elaborate verandahs. Summer villas, which in winter look abandoned, locked and haunted. One of them was. Plato Villa. My ghost wandered there, waiting for the next time Maxine couldn't cope. She'd be back. The problem was, some ghosts had to hitch-hike every day to Tunbridge Wells. I couldn't walk through walls. I could stare at them, I could bang my head on them, even climb them. Forgetting Maxine wasn't working. She couldn't be forgotten; there'd never been enough to forget.

The park stretched out below, tennis courts like disused runways, old leg trees. In the dip, a closed café, and the bandstand puddled in its centre, the town horizon wooded below a grey cowling of sky.

I peered up the cracked mossy drives round the back of each villa. At one, a copper stood with a clipboard looking at an upstairs window. He turned and saw me, seemed on the point of blowing his whistle. A kid's bike leaned against a rusty drainpipe. Emptiness and better days for us all. Times like this leave you faint of mind at all the impenetrable mysteries of privilege and happiness. I was a non-swimmer in this lagoon. Half the houses still had their Tradesman's Entrance. My gawp was a jealous one, I know, and in my face life's ambition had become no more than a move to Tunbridge Wells where I could watch this half-way house day and night for the flicker of its candle, where the streets were paved with second cars and cream tea signs and Maxine's Chesterfield dog-ends.

Along the main road, too, it was hidden Gothic villas, overdraped drawing rooms where the maid always had the day off, and bells rung sharply, pulled by gnarled claws. The halls were full of walking sticks with ducks' heads and horn handles. For all I fucking knew.

I was eighteen, and the stories of William Brown were still my only light on this world, even if I had read David Jones and Ezra Pound and had an affair with a woman twice my age.

I was acting on instinct, so I couldn't have learned much. Except about pain. But pain was instinct too, no? Knowledge of pain creeps up on you, stalking its prey: like me, in my soggy desert boots, my cloak of winter, the days drawing in to show up that light when it came, like whittling a matchstick to nothing but its burnt tip. She hadn't even sent a Christmas card. The windows remained dark.

Then the house began to haunt *me*. As if it was my ghost, rattling through my own empty rooms, vacuum-packed into my memory. The Land Registry Records Office gave the ghost a deepening echo. The house was built in 1869 by Georgius Cordial, who called it Plato Villa. He'd married Isabel Pollenfex the same year. Their joint tomb was in the Old Borough Cemetery. A seated cherub holds a tipped patera. A half-rolled sash has fallen gently over an urn and pedestal. A lunette in low relief shows a pastoral scene: on a postern gate in the foreground, several marble bottles and jars, Cordial's Patent Glycerines & Aspics. The Gothic script below it says: *Risen In Death As In Life — From Nothing*. The Glycerines & Aspics were last in the shops in 1905. Maxine's grandparents inherited the fortune. They weren't landed gentry at all. They'd married the 'from nothings.' Fucking Botts of Bott Hall, capitalist scum, nouveau snob. Hardfarthing Hall was a façade. Even worse, Plato Villa belonged to Miss Flack, who'd been bundled into Colonel Wade's after three hundred empty gin bottles fell out of her cupboard when the district nurse opened it one day.

The day before Christmas Eve was another cold grey afternoon, bad-leg sky, merciless crowds. I hated Christmas. The baggots fake good/bad-will, every utterence a double yoke, their real tempers blistering under the skin, neuralgia at the nativity.

– We're not 'avin no Christmas this year. Carn afford it after payin' your fine. Come out our Christmas box, that. Might 'ave a bit o'chickin' an' a cracker, if yer lucky. Dog woan even get 'er chocs, poor mite...

I didn't want any Christmas, but he said that every year. The subterfuge went on for weeks. Advent unfolded as normal. Nuts put in the sideboard, oranges smelling up the place, one bottle of

Stones Ginger Wine, one Sherry, the tree in the bucket. Come all the Christmas mornings of my life the last present would be unwrapped, but my pile'd only be pencils, hankies from Nan, a grey jumper, a giant pink rubber with *I Must Not Make Big Misteaks* on it.

– Well, boy, that's yer lot till nex' year.

Five minutes later:

– Yep, that's it till nex' year, ay father?

– Yes, thass awl in' it, dawg, ay? Ay, dawg grrr woof-woof, like yer chocs, ay, dawg, ay? Like yer jumper, Enry, ay? Goo on, put it on fer the dog t'see, boy.

The old bag kept her smirk severe.

– 'Aven't yer fergotten somethin', father?

– Oh? 'Ave I, now? Well, yer bedder goo upstairs, Enry; see if I've left anythin' under the bed, ay, dawg?

This year, if they dared, I'd find what I'd asked for under their iron bed. Another fat American novel about affairs with married women in the middle classes. Knowing Maxine'd read it. Knowing she'd chosen me to act out some of the scenes.

– Neck-in-a-knot, old neck-in-a-knot.

The ratbag'd chant at Pinky all right when I unwrap it in front of them and read about the throbbing cocks, wet cunts, come and fucking in the motels and the lodges of Connecticut:

– Sacrificed our guts out fer that … Last Christmas in this 'ouse, mark my words …

I slogged round Tunbridge Wells every day, all day, that week. This was bad enough, without Miss Flack's disapproval. I thought it was time for a revelation or two, and a clue as to Maxine's married name so I could look her up in the phone directory. But Miss Flack was ten-to-the-dozen as usual, still hoping I'd re-join The Chalybeate Poets. Numbers were down, apparently.

– I understand your reluctance, chum. But I daresay they're harmless enough in their own way. Quite charming, some of them, I'm sure, even if standards do vary or waver, I'm afraid. All keen as mustard, just not as sharp. Of course, everyone writes nowadays, so we have got some of the younger set come in, you see. We've a pig farmer and his wife from Speldhurst. Extremely nice. But we must have a constant supply of young blood. Keep us on our toes, hmmmmm?

Well, I thought, that made Maxine a whole poetry society of her own. Poetry & Pints. Transfusional Verse.

Once again the stupid game was to try and find a way to get her into the sentence.

– Why, uhm, why've you never asked your, uhm, your niece?

– ...the fortnightly meetings can be threadbare occasions. Of course, I can't get to as many meetings as I'd like either, on account of my legs, you know. Mr Munns used to drive me down when he could, poor dear, before his squint worsened and he couldn't really control the thing, colliding with Belisha Beacons. And the other day, very unfortunately, when I did actually walk somewhere, I had an unpleasant episode in The Grove, just a week after Miss Monks had her lucky escape, too. A man walking his dog scared the would-be muggers away. No such luck, in my case. Enjoying my short stroll home from a meeting, or was it from Mr Biggs talk on heather farming? Lord, memory like a thingmajig. I do hope I haven't unfairly associated the poetry competition with that unemployed plumber... He leapt out on me, you see, from behind a beech tree. Waved his spanner in my face. Ran off with my knitting bag and about ten shillings in copper. Told me he'd just argued with his girlfriend and failed his City & Guilds. Now, where was I? Oh, yey, wouldn't you like to publish a pamphlet of your own one day, chum?

– Well, uhm, what I...

– You've not got enough yet, I suspect, no. Well, never mind. Some of the Chalybeates have scriven their lives to the bone and never come near. Once or twice, something rises. Being on the elderly side, as you know dear, they have their losses, and we tend to get sarcophogii in every stanza. You can't blame us for that. Poor Ambrose did lose his cat, dear man, but how he got it into that sarcophogus is anyone's guess. Sorry, you said something, chum?

– I'm in love with your niece. I want to send her a poem and a Christmas card ... I've lost her address...

– No can do, Henry. Sorry mate, but I think you've bought enough harm on yourself. I did have some tiny inkling, you see. I'd rather you didn't go bothering her this Christmas. Even if I felt so inclined, I couldn't possibly interfere. You must accept it should never have happened. Bad idea, moment of folly. I'm afraid my niece has behaved deplorably. Hard facts, chum, but you have to accept that you mean nothing to her and that's my last word. Come back to the Chalybeates and we'll forget it. There's Alan Brownjohn judging this year. Now then, more tea in the pot...

Outside, the carols on the dampened air were like the voices of the drowned. Blinkin' City. Sore afraid. In class 9, Old Trotmann had pushed me in the swimming pool and I half-drowned/half-dog-paddled the width, such was the momentum of the fear and the panic. Trotmann thought I'd swum it, i.e. not touched bottom. It was only twenty feet wide, but he gave me a swimming certificate for the width. That's what it sounded like in Tunbridge Wells after Miss Flack's little riot act, chlorinated hell-water in my ears as I pissed myself in my orange trunks. Lights, banners, nativities, glitter, heels. A migraine day. I was drowning. Definitely touched bottom. The loneliness of a twenty-foot swimmer, but I'd got that certificate which allowed me to cross the width of society, a certificate falsely made out by Maxine Pollenfex. So swim I fuckin' would. I'd find her. We'd live at Plato Villa and on my tomb it would say *Risen from Nothing*.

Even at birth they'd made the same mistake, the Registrar of Births at Cranbrook. They put me in the working class with a single blue scratch of an old Parker pen, just one bald entry beside the ultimate question: Father's Occupation. Rat Catcher. Yes, I was jealous of all these well to-do shoppers within walking distance of their houses, family gatherings I could only guess at. I was George's boy, all right. I'd got the heirloom in my pocket, an inferiority ring I kept so shiny it was wearing down to a strip of wire. I was the ratcatcher now, out to catch the queen rat when she came back to the black hole she liked to crawl in when the poison was down. The poison pen that writes the poison poem. The old bag was right. Maxine'd bought shame on us. She'd made me ashamed of myself, too. Forget the pain, now. It was the crying shame I wanted her to know about. Good old copper-bottomed Victorian shame.

She wasn't there among the shoppers. I did the department stores twice a day. I hung about the avocado pears till they went rotten. In the street there were drunks and revellers, office parties spilling out the bistros. Postmen collected the last delivery before Christmas.

I toiled up Mt Pleasant Road towards the bus stop, swerving to avoid the swaying men with tinsel round their necks. One of them saw me:

– Weyyyyyyyyyyy-heyyyyyyyy, gloomy boots. Chrissmas ain' a

funeral.

He blew a plastic trumpet in my ear and as I ran off he puked up a colourful voluntary. I saw a girl bent retching outside Chiesman's, all her co-workers and the under-manager with their name and rank tabs stood waiting for her to finish. She was saying sorry-sorry between heaves, and even Merry Christmas as the crowd gathered to see what was going on.

I was out of synch. I wasn't even in this world now. I was just a bobbin-boy the day before they invented Spinning Jenny. Another 10p tea in the Zippy, scanning every face which passed by. I was rolling up dog-ends, owing to the bus-fares, and Fatty Stamp finally caught me out. I'd been using my expired college bus pass for at least a month. I'd better get a hundred Winstons under that poxy tree Christmas morning or I'd be filching the old man's Tom Thumbs. One last look at Plato Villa and then the six o' clock bus home… That's when I saw it.

The outside light was on, a car door slammed – a dark car, but not the maroon Austin Maxine. The man said:

– Have you got…

But I couldn't catch the rest and the woman was indistinct, half inside the front door where the hall light was on. They'd just arrived. But who were they? The man made quick soldier-like movements, flexed his shoulders, picked up a bag. He was wearing a crombie with a scarf tucked inside. I had four minutes to leg it to the bus.

The 254 ticked over at the War Memorial. The driver was Fatty Stamp as usual, one of the old man's enemies. Any enemy of the old man was a friend of mine, but not in this case. Fatty Stamp tried to fault my ticket, some slight pocket damage.

– It's a return, I said.

– I know that, sonny Jim. Just take care of it next time.

I chose the same seat as always, left, one in front of the wheel hub, behind a woman and her teenage daughter.

– We done rather well din' we, Rachel? the woman said. Better v'n last year.

She opened her purse and took out some coins.

– Look at them. Juss bin issued. Musta god'em in Marks. You c'n av 'm, put 'em in yer money box.

Rachel wiped the condensation from the window with her gloves. Her mother went on:

– I got 'im some 'ankies. 'E uses a lot, dun'e? Are you lookin'?
Now, where'd I put that tin? Oh, 'ere it is, see? Bluebird Toffees,
look: good make. Tin's nice to use fer summing…

Fatty Stamp revved up and pulled away; the noise drowned out
Rachel's mum. She was just like my old bag, her voice clicking some
automatic switch which made me lean over and nearly say: I doan
want no more bloody 'ankies.

Next morning I couldn't get a lift. I had to get to Plato Villa, life
or death now. Three hours, frostbit thumb, looking for all the
world like Henry Chambers, six months suspended, twenty pound
damages for the broken window. Well, at least I managed to spoil
a few last-minute Christmas shopping trips. All the passing cars
breaking the speed limit to get away from me. Maybe I shouldn't
have stood hitching on the very spot where the pigs nabbed me,
opposite Parson Potter's driveway. Pity the Good Samaritan himself
hadn't pootled out in his Allegro to test the scriptures. God never
sent a car to pick me up.

Reading Sherlock Holmes and Maigret had sharpened up my
observational powers, though. I'd noticed that Plato Villa had had
a phone line put in since my time. So I gave up thumbing and went
up the GPO. There were two phoneboxes outside the village Post
Office. One stank of piss-flavoured mints, the other of wet fag ash.
There were other phoneboxes in Hawkhurst, outposts where you
made bomb scares or shouted on windy nights about your bad legs.
I'd never used the phoneboxes much, but when I had it was always
a thumping heart emergency, a self-pity night, *there's a bomb under
the Girls' Grammar School speech day stage.* I didn't know what
else you used one for. Phone the gas, order logs? The glass was
smashed at the one outside the Post Office. There was traffic at the
lights, it was midday, so maybe Maxine was pulping her avocado for
the new poet in her life. How many poets wore crombies, though?
Or was it Gerald, and they'd come for Christmas? That was my
hope. I'd be down that chimney with my box of chocolate shames.
I'd be waiting up The Grove with my poetry spanner to mug Maxine
when she tried out her new galoshes on Boxing Day.

I dialled directory enquiries. And this time, at last, I had a number
for M. Pollenfex, Plato Villa. I started to dial, with no idea of what
to say. The phone in the box next door started ringing. I must have

dialled up the box next door, then. I slammed my receiver down but the other phone kept ringing. I knew who that was. Half the village had talked to him, this John from Tunbridge Wells, a sex maniac, been doing filthy calls for years. I waited till it stopped, then dialed again quick before mine rang.

The bloke in the crombie answered. Short, sharp:
– Yes?
– Oh, good morning, is that Mr Pollenfex?
– What do you want?
– Mr Gerald Pollenfex?
– No it's not. Gerald O'Connor. What is it you want?
– Would Mrs Pollenfex be there by any chance?
– No she would not. I'm here alone. Now what is it you want? I'm in a hurry to get back to London.
– Well, you fucking arsehole in a crombie, I'm watching you. My name's John from Tunbridge Wells and I was a virgin till your wife fucked me, right where you're standing now. I tell you, if you're still standing there in ten minutes I'm gonna kill you and your bit of crumpet…

He laughed. Maybe John had already rung him. He wasn't the least bit scared. Like this woman in Hawkhurst John rang one night, Shirley up the Esso Garage. He says: what colour knickers are you wearing? She says: 'old on a mo', let me fetch a chair… You dirty cow, he says, and rings off. Gerald was lighting a cigar, probably.
– Well, if it's not young Henry, he says. I know all about you. You smell, apparently. Or was that Dan? Ah, I know: you're the one who still lives with his dreadful parents, aren't you? All I have to do is phone the Police, you know…

Right in my ear, as if he was standing there. I looked round with the hair standing up on my head. Then I slammed that phone down so quick and ran out of there so fast I left my gloves behind. The other phone was still ringing.

113

nineteen

Me and the old man were building up for our big finale too, only this one went a bit better than expected. He blamed his angina on me. 'Don't upset yer father' was the new family proverb. The doctor said he had to avoid all stress, and the old man said how could he when a son like me lived under the same roof. My own heart was sound, true, up its sleeve, in its right place. I imagined the old man's like an Albert on a rusty pocket chain, stuck on the eleventh hour, whereas mine was always at ten to three. So there we were, stuck in different times, winding each other up.

Christmas came and went as the family tree sat it out in its galvanised pail disguised with gift wrapping. The old man stood beside it as if he was the lumberjack sent out to fell it. Just a poor sapling. Threatened to burn it, up the back garden. He kept saying 'who luvs yer, baby' and couldn't wait to get back to work. He smote and sucked a Tom Thumb cigar and rattled the tub of *Good Boy* chocs we always got the dog. Pinky, the excitable asthmatic runt he'd saved from a drowning in Alf Butters's rain tub back in the fifties. Pinky tore at the gold wrapping for her master's amusement, asthmatic splutter re-living the moment when Mr Butters tied her up in a sack with six other chicken legs and shoved it under with a broomstick. He drove Pinky to the edge while his Tom Thumb melted a hole in the nylon chair cover. That made three of us with a motive, two with an alibi. Me, Pinky and the sapling.

He turned on me last of all. After breakfast, the day of Epiphany, his life-long *All-Bran* and a fag on the bog, then his wash in the kitchen sink, braving the cold water, drying himself in his singlet. I was on my way upstairs.

– Get back down 'ere, boy. I wanna word with you. I don't know what the blinkin' 'eck you're up to, but I'd put a stop to it now. Before it turns bad again. Haven't you done enough damage? And clear them books off the chair. Yer mother shouldn' aff ter run round after you day-in day-out. An' clean the mud off yer boots in future before bringin' 'em in the shed.

– What's the point? I said. I use 'em every day and put 'em on newspaper.

– Gawd, boy, use some savvy an' do as yer told. And tell me the truth, for once. Are you seeing that married jane again?

– What jane?

– Don't try my patience, lad. We see how you've bin the last few weeks. Don't know if yer comin' or goin' any more. We know the signs, we're not stupid. Messing where you've no business to be. Now, move yerself, I wanna get that tree away.

I'd been waiting for just such an opportunity. Chris Kirby said everyone at the depot knew about it. The old man was giving Edie Burns one in the back of his Hillman Minx. She was this spinster with a squint the old man had just taught to drive, lived up the road next to Basil Smith. This Edie, she must've been fifty and now she wanted to start driving round all the village WIs in a Morris Minor with her sister, Miss Burns, who looked about ninety and'd got bad feet and ought to've smelled of piss under her travel blanket but didn't, quite, though she croaked like a pelican and smelled of camphor. Edie was a titless wonder, a goofy cow in a green cardie and a tartan skirt, and I'd even seen her in a clear plastic mac with the sun shining through it onto her handbag. I thought Edie worked in the bank, but I'd seen her sneaking up the posh house paths along Highate with a black bag and a nursey face like she'd come to wipe arses. She gave you the shivers, that beaky nose and eyes like pools of cat-sick. She was out of place down our road too, a bit genteel, fallen on hard times maybe, thought she ought to live up Highgate in a weatherboard house, not with Basil Smith next door, with his fucking ferrets and fag-ends over the fence, match fishing on Sundays, up the Legion most evenings where my old man pulled his pints part-time, probably to pay for Edie's Parma-Violets or her silence. The old man said Edie was too respectable to live next door to Mrs Smith who went to the chip van in slippers and a fag-dab on her lip, like someone else we both lived with, of course.

– Oh yeah? I said. And what about you and Edie, hypocrite? Teaching her to screw an' all, are yer? The L-Plate bedroom? You're the talk of the fuckin' depot, you arsehole. All the blokes...

He would've cracked me one on the side of the head if the other baggot hadn't come in the back door with her peg bag. He managed to get his last words in:

– Don't you open that filthy trap o' yours t'your mother, or blow me, boy, I'll get you later … And wrap yer chutty-gum in paper 'fore you put it in the bin. Right, let's get that damned tree away.

As the tree began its final journey towards the back door, it shed its needles. It wasn't going without a scrap, but the old woman had the vacuum cleaner standing by. I went upstairs and looked out the toilet window. The old bastard was lying on his back in the mud. It fuckin' worked. The tree was just finishing him off. I heard the vacuum cleaner sucking up its needles in the front room. I wanted to run away, shin down the drainpipe, flee up the village, down Little Switzerland. Anywhere, to wait till this was all over, till our last feelings for each other were out of the way, back in the vacuum we'd grown used to.

The hoover stopped. I ran downstairs because I couldn't let her discover the murderer. She was in a tuss over the flex, yanking at the knots and singing with her teeth:

I love youuuuuuuuu
Yes I dooooooooooo
Oh how I hate youuuuuuuuuuuuuuuuuu
It's a siiiiiiiiiinnnnnnn to tellllllllllllll a flippin' lie …

– There's some trouble in the back garden, I said. Do I, uhm, call the ambulance?

I saw the rest from the toilet window, too. The neighbours, neither of whom would see another Christmas, led the old woman away and hid the corpse under a blanket. I locked the toilet door when the ambulance arrived and bocked up my breakfast when they lifted him onto the stretcher.

Wow, I thought, the hired sapling did it. We did it, we killed him on the Day of Epiphany. Special, that. It made up for finding out that Maxine had betrayed me to the Crombie, laughed at me with that git who was using Plato Villa as a knocking shop himself. But there'd be consequences and interruptions now, and christ knows what. Maxine might have to wait a couple of weeks. This was a real death.

I fucked off to Tunbridge Wells while the neighbours comforted the widow and the ambulance dithered for the doctor. There was an awful moment hitching. I'd got as far as Flimwell when the ambulance passed me on the way to the Kent & Sussex with his body in the back. He wouldn't even give me a lift to hell with him.

In town I went looking for Basher. She was Polish. She wasn't my girlfriend, I'd met her in the Zippy Bar a month back while taking all those teas in between vigils at Plato Villa. She was looking for a husband so she could 'get visa and go to United States.' She said I was 'loneliest person' she knew. She said: I'm lonely too, I hate my job. She was a Marlboro addict and a chambermaid in one of those big residential hotels in London Road. A couple of times we'd gone to her room down in the basement. She brought me tea from the kitchens, we talked about whatever she was reading. Then once, in my lonely clothes, I did a striptease – which sort of baffled both of us, but she found it amusing. She didn't seem interested in sex but she gave me a hand shandy and I came all over the ceiling then put my clothes on and got the bus back to Hawkhurst. It helped at the time. She wasn't pretty. She'd got a big nose, hairy legs … nice lips, though. Anyway, the day the bastard died she'd looked for me in the Zippy, sat down and said she couldn't find a husband anywhere. I'd said try the fuckin' poetry society – anywhere but the Zippy. She could see I was in a state, excited, so I told her I'd just killed my dad. You know? – I was his Angina of Death. She loved it, then said she wanted to lose her virginity and she'd chosen me after all.

We went back to her room. She borrowed a johnny from Ricardo the Columbian waiter. We swigged some vodka. But it was all knees and dry as drought and we didn't know what we were doing. I thought Maxine had made me experienced. I suppose all the feelings were so different I couldn't see any common ground. Then Basher said all right, stop, that's enough, go, get your bus, leave me alone.

It got worse. That night the phone rang at 2.30 am. It wouldn't stop ringing, which terrified and rattled the old woman, who'd been given a Valium sledgehammer up the arm. I had no idea who it was. My best guess was John or the Crombie. I opened my door and found the baggot in her valium nightmare, a blue 75-milligram panic, saying: it must be the hospital. He'd woken up, he wasn't dead, they'd spent fourteen hours doing mouth-to-mouth and he'd risen from the blanket and the sapling had confessed and grassed me up…

She went down and picked the phone up in her pink slippers and bunions.

– Father? Is that you? What! Who's that! What yer ringing 'im now for? Don't you know what time it is? Don't yer know who's dead, yer strumpet?

Then it was my turn for derangement. It was Maxine: she'd heard of my bereavement or was ringing to say Gerald had dropped dead on Christmas Eve too, at Plato Villa, with the phone in his hands and his crumpet weeping bullets. I nearly broke my kneck jumping down the stairs and wrestling the phone off the grieving baggot before she slammed it down and ruined my last chance ever.

– Maxine?

It wasn't Maxine. It was Basher.

The old woman said I better not be long about it or there'd be consequences, what with yer father not yet in his grave. Oh yeah? Coming round, was he, to swipe his ectoplasm across the back of my leg ? I put the receiver to my ear.

– Why did you do it? Basher shouted. Why, why, why? Tell me, you pig. You are pig with brain, you are sex maniac, and your mother is common woman.

– I can't talk now, I said. It's the middle of the night. This is a house of mourning and my mother can hear from her bedroom.

– I don't care for bloody parents. Why did you do it?

– Why did you ask me? You asked me.

– You didn' have to do it. I wanted you to make love. It was disgusting. I feel nothing. I am ashamed. I'm Catholic girl from Nowa Huta.

– Me too... But she'd hung up. I left the phone off the hook. The old bastard could send a telegram if he woke up.

Before the funeral I divided the chocolate lanterns into three and gave the spare share to Pinky. It was her turn next. The vet'd said she mustn't eat chocolate. I buried her in a plastic bag where the 'dead' tried growing celery once. Then it was time to think of leaving home and growing up, starting out, picking up the trail. Maxine would feel differently about someone who didn't live with his parents any more, specially when she found out that Gerald was playing away.

The council said that if I went, the old woman'd have to move into a widow's bungalow a few doors up. There was an empty one ready and waiting, next to Hector Haunt. Be less rent.

– Small mercy, she said.

She was called Mercy, and she was small. There were dog roses, nice, over the porch trellis. Miss Roach died there in November, left her linen peg-bag hanging on a nail from the clothes pole and a pair of rusty secateurs in the grass.

At the funeral I was dry-eyed. Still managed to retch behind a tree as the dirt filled him in, though. Edie filled his grave with tears and Small Mercy just stared at her with a face like a bulldog. No point cremating him, iron man, you'd have to put him in a smelter and say: Dad's gone to the big scrap yard in the sky. Or Dr Beeching took him, hard as British rails he was.

They were finished, the bottled-up, pickled years with nothing worth preserving. The end of a family life spent in fruitless pursuit of respectability and obsession with appearences. In a house where visitors never darkened the door. 'Betters' never came to council houses, unless they had affairs with me.

I tried for a month to get a bedsit in Tunbridge Wells. But you had to have a job with luncheon vouchers, or plastic bags of money from dealing microdots and Red Leb. You had to be a Summerhill cory. I knew all that, but having to learn it over again was a blow in the guts. At least in Hawkhurst the derision had stopped, or become tolerant. I could walk in four directions without being noticed now. Small Mercy tip-toed about like she was scared that the dust she'd just swiped would wake up and fight back. Everything was regular to the split second again. You clocked on for the set-piece of life. Even the persecution had its time and place. Nothing had changed since 1955, except the paint on the front door and the empty chair.

I'd saved up all the advantages of adulthood too, resisted against all the goading till it was time and I was free of him. Gonna vote Henry? he'd say. Not till you're dead, I'd think. The whole road voted Labour except him and her. She wouldn't ever vote again, not even for Ted Heath, their favourite gonk. Try a Tom Thumb, have a whisky, round of golf boy, round of golf and grow fucking up ...

After the funeral, no flowers please, only weeds, me and Small Mercy went back to the house, handed round some fish-paste sarnies to the half-dead, then cleared the effects without another word, like cleaning up after an act of God. We obliterated every trace of his life: every nut, bolt and letter-opener, every ashtray, pipe-cleaner and eye-bath. Thank Christ they buried him with his teeth glued in. It was as if we'd conspired in the perfect murder, only all the benefits went sour when we realised we could've done it ten years ago. She did the bedroom herself, sobbing as she swept him out, bagged him into rag-and-bone. I filled a hot water bottle and went to bed with cotton wool in my ears. Did Maxine know that real death left a taste of avocado pith?

In the morning I went downstairs and ate breakfast in my usual place. The paperboy still delivered the *Daily Express*. Went straight onto the pile beside Pinky's box in the shed. United Friendly sent George H Chambers a cheap brown envelope. The day began like any other in that house, sunrise behind a cloud against the one wall without a window. Yes, it was time to fill the gaping hole with voting, pipe-smoking and whisky ... I didn't know. Where was that vision you had to have of yourself? That had been the first thing murdered in no. 51 during the slaughtering of the innocents.

Mr Miles New & Secondhand came before my tea went cold to look over the furniture which wasn't wanted up the bungalow. Old walrus man in a checked suit, tea-stained 'tache, smelled of cheese on toast and still whistled tunes from World War One.

– Cor, he said, still got this? Inky-pinky-parly-vous...

The desk in the front room.

– Did you know, Henry, that I supplied this – oooh, let's see now, blimey, musta bin all 'o twenty-five year ago. Long before you ever come to this 'ouse, young fella.

I followed him from room to room with Small Mercy standing at the kitchen window wiping her nose saying she didn't want none of it bar a table and chair to rest her bones on and drink her last cup of tea.

– Dear oh dear, dear me no, tut-tut Mercy, he'd say. That won't be doing you any good now will it...

Upstairs he whistled *Mademoiselle from Armantières* and said:

– Now then, Hennery, what have we here? Wardrobe, dressing table, iron bed...

I pointed out the chest of drawers on the landing and he bent over and sniffed it.

– Not much cop wivout all the knobs, Hennery.

Then we went in my bedroom. It hadn't been decided what I'd do, or where my furniture, which wasn't mine, would go.

– And where will you go, Hennery, if yer don't mind my askin'? I mean, I can see y've packed, like. Mind you, a piece of furniture or two might come in handy.

I hadn't packed, I just didn't own anything. I'd already sold it all to Mr Miles to fund my bus fares and fags to Tunbridge Wells and he knew it.

– I don't know, I said. Something'll, uhm, turn up.

– Indeed it will, he said. You can take the flat above my draper's if it suits.

– I'm trying to get a bedsit in Tunbridge Wells.

– Tut-tut. You'll be lucky if yer find a room in the Wells. I know you've had yer troubles, lad, but I'm sure you're not an ... er... Between you an' me I had to chuck that Macey fella out last week, caw-dear! Hahaha. Pig in a poke, that boy. You're respectable, Henry, despite a few – shall we say – hiccoughs. Decent people, yer mum and dad. I can see yer kept yer bedroom neat and tidy...

Neat and tidy, my Ada. Small Mercy went through it daily with her dust detective. The only thing she'd never tried to scrub off was the blood on Maxine-glass.

I'd been six when we moved down from no. 9 to 51, ran alongside the handcart with the two beds on it, jumping on the floorboards of my empty bedroom, gazing at the clustered flowers stencilled along the walls. They were still there.

– The drapers is furnished, Mr Miles said, but Macey swiped the bed. I can drop yawn off if yer like, shall I?

– No no, I said. You don't have to do that...

– No bother, me lad. I've known yer parents since they first come t'Awkh'st with nothing but the gleam in their eye.

– But I've had that bed since I was five.

– I know Henry, I know. I sold it t'yer dad. Right, now then, one wardrobe, one high-chair...

We heard Small Mercy filling the kettle, hoping she was back to normal.

– She all right down there, your mum?

– I dunno.

– Terrible thing, terrible, losing someone after s'long. See a lot of passing away in my line of business. Always follow the hobituaries, mind, visit the widows, bit o' furniture here and there, Hennery. Never forgot a piece all me life. Caw, ged it back in the end I do, bit worse fer wear but there's always plenty of life left in a good bit of work. Blessed if I don't remember the day you were born, too. Just 'appened to lay my hands on a nice pink cot fer nex t' nuthin' rottin' away in me bargain basement. Not still about, is it, Hennery? Back in fashion now, them oak cots with the rockers...

By the middle of February I was living alone above the draper's, looking across at the chemist's. Small Mercy had become another old bag behind a net curtain, banging on the window at whippersnappers kicking footballs against the kerb. Right through her head, it went.

twenty

Parson Potter was in your kitchen quick as Mr Miles. He had an eye for a nice bit of grief. His whipper-in called round before my old man'd pushed up his first daisy. Son of Dust, thumbing my door buzzer, thinking I was easy meat now. The lost sheep of scripture in his Good News Bible.

– I can really feel the pain in you, Hen.

He wasn't even a Jesus freak anymore. When he said hey, let's have some sounds, he put Handel's Messiah on. He said he'd taken the righteous path to salvation. Milky coffee, scripture study three evenings a week, and a job.

– I'm truly sorry to hear you say that, man.

Sorry because I'd rebuffed his condolences and said:

– I'm glad he's dead. He was a cunt.

– Look, man, I'm on your side, but this is pain that forgiveness heals.

– You should be pleased, I said. Supposing you'd come round here and said Jesus and his dad, God, had taken him for his garden, they only take the best – well, I'd have to smash your fucking head in, wouldn't I?

– There's a truth there, man. Indeedy.

He'd started to pronounce half of what he said in American. Words like *boodiful*.

– It's boodiful working with wood. A craft is rilly a spridual thing, man.

Nowadays he wore those denim carpenters' jeans with the big yellow stitching, like lines painted on the road. Lumberjack shirts, chunky boots, suede hat and a wax jacket. He said he'd helped make my old man's coffin. They'd let him sand it down by hand. He was apprenticed to the chippy back of Mr Miles yard. If I'd stood tiptoe on my bog seat I might've seen him taking his milky coffee break, thermos on the upturned coffin lid. He was proud of his tools, Stanley's best, proud of the brass-tipped rule sticking out of his yellow-stitched ruler pocket. He'd got nerve, walking in there and saying he wanted to learn carpentry. I had grudging respect for that. He knew who he was. He'd've just marched on Maxine's door with a banner and said: now look here, lady… The chippies are the gum-shield and shin-pad back four in the Hawks second team, too. Ex-Swattenden hards who didn't think sanding coffins and dressers was 'boodiful' or 'spridual.' They called him Dusty. He had a long copper beard, too.

He'd stopped by on his way home for his workman's tea. Once he'd called it supper. There was another boy in my year called it supper, and he got his ears twisted for that. Son of Dust had it all worked out. Three years carpentry by day till he was in the Guild. Three years scripture homework with Parson Potter in the evenings. Then he'd set sail on the Mayflower to the New World where he'd build a wooden church among the Bourbon-swilling Virginian lumberjacks. In the meantime, I was under his pastoral care, part of his sandwich course.

He already had that all-seeing aura. A new habit too, sucking his lips like he could taste the holy spirit. He'd got a new front tooth, so it was probably just the chocolate under the palette, a trick of the trade Parson Potter taught him. He chewed his nails, too. His fingertips were snub and baby-pink. But he was company, I craved company, and he knew it. He slipped through with split-second timing, as if he could see me too if he stood tiptoe on his latest coffin lid. It was that vulnerable time, the five o' clock shadow when you get in from the encounterless walk, the diurnal repetition of your failure to put it to rest. When you sit at the poker table shuffling your pack of lies to yourself. I'd just been up the cemetery too, for a Morris-Minor dance on the cunt's grave.

– Look, man, I won't take up any more of your precious time, Son of Dust said, but you're invided out tonight. No preachy vibes, you know? No heavy stuff, just fellowship, it's a pardy, tastes, sounds. A kinda send-off, you know? Brim's going to the States. The Parson's sending him to Bible college. He'd really love for you to be there. It's a rilly impordant moment, he might never come back… Meet at the Manse, yeah? Half-six…

Well, I was never one to deny another fascist missionary a groovy 'so long' if he promised never to come back. I needed some decent sausage rolls and ham sandwiches too. I'd lived alone for two weeks. I was getting nine pounds forty-nine and the rent paid. Three

124

nights a week over the chip shop, pastie and chips. Wayne's Dad gave me extra scrapings and I added my own baked beans and sausage and watched the late horror or some highlights on my rented Rediffusion. I'd borrowed Small Mercy's *Woman's Realm* cookbook and could do an œuf boulangère. All you did was fry some chips, put them in a glass bowl with fried onions, crack an egg over it and pop it in the Baby Belling for fifteen minutes. Mixed herbs optional. They were better smoked, you could really get a buzz. The nine quid had run out with three days to go.

The Potters had moved out of their chapelside bungalow and into the big Manse. A childless couple with ten empty rooms. It was nearer the shops than Dust's Manse, set back from the road with a gravel drive and hidden by thick laurels. Straight out of the William books.

– Welcome! Hi, Henry, great to see you.

He was on the doormat in his shiney Tuf shoes. Yellow frosted glass, modern Bible script framed under glass, his wife a beige mist and a flit of handshake that could've been a yellow duster. I didn't know what it was about Baptists, but they thrived alongside bright, polished wood. The chapel with its new wooden organ in proclamation yellow, the pews like varnished open-heart coffins. The Manse was varnished like an angel's yacht too, all these wooden crosses on every wall and the smell of unmade lives, wart lotion and fly spray. Did I want a cup of tea and a biscuit? Hang on, wait a minute. Am I early? Where was everyone?

– Come through, Henry…

I was in his study, the door clicked behind me, a chapel-panelled door you'd never find again if you wanted to flee in panic. The study continued the general theme of crosses, scripture, and those glossy volumes with padded blue covers only Parsons read. Alcoholics Anonymous who-dunnits, Salvation Army thrillers. Prayers for the modern novel. It was sterile comfort, the man lacked nothing but wore it all drip-dry, teetotal and elasticated. All the texture of a public library in Salt Lake City. Even the curtains were Airtex. He was clean-cut but there was dandruff, boney jaw, NHS specs, a gold signet ring, everything tucked in its place and pasty, second shave of the day shining in the striplight, stigmata of Gillette along the jawline.

– Thanks for coming, Hen. It's great to see you again. Great, good, okay. Look, I just thought we'd all benefit from a litttle chat, a friendly man-to-man. We're men, Henry, we're people, caring people. Then we'll go on to Brim Stone's appreciation together. More uplifted, I hope. How do you feel, Henry?

– I don't understand, I said. Where's the party?

– Down the chapel, of course.

– Oh, the bastard.

A crippled smile from the Parson, a flat thin Charlie Browner instead of a lie, instead of owning up to his complicity. He was wearing a flower tie and his blazer was hooked over the back of his chair. His shirt was yellow, like his goolies. The lapel badge on his jacket was the christian fish.

– I heard about your father, of course. I'm very sorry for you. It's a hard world, Henry, and you've had your fare share of woe. We've prayed for you, I'd like you to know that. God's on his way to you, Henry. Do you believe that?

He was reading this out from a piece of paper hidden behind his prayer book, surely. What did he know about fair share of woe? This man used to be a shoe salesman in Bromley and could've walked into any shoe salesman job the world over like it was a slip-on gusset fit. So who tricked him into the Chapel when he was happy selling B width soles instead of saving them?

– You know, Henry, when I was your age I was tempted too, sorely tempted. I wasn't a saint – oh, not by any means. I haven't always carried the Lord in here…

He slapped his rib-cage, then re-adjusted his tie pin. The Lord in his rib-cage, like a rabbit or what?

– I've had my scrapes, and Valerie and I struggled in our early years…

This was embarrassing me. They were in their early thirties. Valerie Potter was barren by choice, black leg-hairs flattened under cheap tights, silver green cardigans and silly short coats above her cold red knees. You could keep a bottle of milk fresh inside her coat, and she always stood where you would put the fridge. She backed him up in all his lies about the Lord, those monthly payments of two hundred pounds into their Barclays account. The cans of petrol, the kidnapped souls, all the Lord's helping hand, everything they bought on the always-always.

– Sonny told me something of your tribulations over this married woman...

– He what?

– We're your friends, Henry. Sonny's genuinely worried about where you're heading. We'd like to help you through it, if you'd let us. Trust us, trust the Lord...

– Which one's the door? I said standing in front of a row of bloody panels.

– Come on, lad, that won't get you anywhere. Now sit down, pray with me.

– Play with you? You've gotta be fuckin' joking.

I'd had to take Pinky to the vet once. There was a locum, grey-bearded bloke who spoke about three words a minute. While he was stuffing his finger up Pinky's arse looking for split ends, he coaxed out of me the fact that I wrote poetry. He opened a drawer, and there was a poem in it he'd just written on foolscap, between dogs, about some bloke coming in wet with rain, through the French windows. The last line was something like: There, that wasn't so hard, was it, now... As I'm reading it he touches me with the finger he'd had up Pinky's arse, and it was cold, a Sidney-bone.

– I'm very grateful that your father sent you here...

I was out of there so fast I gave Pinky one of her fits. The vet chased after us, shouting:

– Oh, the poor dog, the poor dog...

The Parson had his cold white hand on my arm next. It smelled as if it had been up the Lord's arse too. His breath was stale mouthwash before fish supper.

– Your father sent you here, Henry. He didn't die in vain. The Lord is our father, now. Pray with me, Henry, just once. Our Father... You won't regret it, you'll feel your weight rise up and leave the room, like smoke up a chimney.

– I didn't come with any weights. I smoke roll-ups now.

It was as if I had to keep thinking up the jokes to ward off hypnotic powers or the effects of Micky Finn.

I found the door first lurch. That bloody Valerie Parsnip was eavesdropping. She leapt up the stairs, white as a sheet with her christian fish a frozen cod on the five-star freezer setting. Then I saw why. The Parson had come up behind me with one of his wooden crosses in his hand – like a bleedin' camping mallet, it was. It looked as if he was going to crack me over the skull with it. His eyes had gone green. Something came out of his mouth, a plasm of tongues like he was swilling the mouthwash anew:

– Eesham, guzhbam, shoesham, leave thish man alone...

A door slammed upstairs where Parsnip locked herself in the bedroom.

– Shoesham, booshik, evil spirit leave Henry Chambers in the name of Jesus...

He had me in a stranglehold and the mallet was thrust up my back. I did a Sid Catt and stamped as hard as I could on the Parson's foot. He yelped:

– Aaahhhh fuckin' jesus christ almighty, my toes, he said and hopped off me. Didn't have the size nine steel toe-capped in stock that week. The holy mallet clattered to the ground too so I gave it a free kick from thirty yards.

– Devil, get thee gone!

– Fuck you, Parson. I'm going.

Outside, there was a high moon and hard glass-cutting stars. The gravel in the drive was frozen together underfoot so I couldn't grab a handful and chuck it at Potter's front door.

It was time to get moving, take this void home to its rightful owner. I could deal with the Parson later. I'd got Maxine's number from the London phonebook in the post office. I'd just lacked the courage to dial it up to now. G. O'Connor, 27 Chorley Crescent, Notting Hill. Six rings and he picked up, the Crombie's voice, that contempt from Christmas Eve, absolutely unmistakable, being bloody was his birthright. Just to make sure, I asked for Mrs Pollenfex in disguise, the twang of my own birthright.

– She's at some poetry thing, he said, like she had a jamrag on.

– So you're all alone, are you, Captain? Look out the window, I'm in the phonebox opposite.

– Oh, I don't think you are, Henry. Maxine's out with her latest little versifier right now, practising couplets, I shouldn't wonder. Take it on the chin, lad, she's not worth it...

– Well, I'm coming for her tomorrow, you fucking tell her that...

– Be my guest, he said. You put one foot on my doorstep and I'll break your legs, understood?

We both slammed the phone down simultaneously.

twenty-one

The Pig & Whistle was just an ordinary looking pub in Notting Hill. A sandwich board outside said: *DJs Wanted. Auditions start 6pm.* That was like in five minutes time. I didn't see why I couldn't be a DJ. This seemed like the lucky break I'd been waiting for, one of Miss Flack's 'green crows.' Notting Hill, and it might even be Maxine's local boozer. I'd call myself DJ Devil, that sounded really ace. I could do the lingo, I listened to Radio Caroline a lot even if I hated the music. Leo Sayer and … all them. Christ, a year back, I used to listen to Stockhausen and things like Penderetski's Threnody for the Victims of Hiroshima. I'd read Lit Crit for fun and watched Tarkovsky films and listened to third programme plays. I'd even written to the BBC and asked for copies of the scripts. As recently as autumn I'd wanted to write like Beckett and paint like Kandinsky and live like Kafka and Rimbaud. At Christmas I'd still read John Updike novels as if Maxine had written them herself about us. But post-Maxine had eventually turned into bedtime with yellow crime novels out of the library and Wings' latest single. The Renaissance was over. Henry the Eighth had burned the libraries.

The disco podium was a few yards from the bar. A tiny dance floor with pub tables to the side, crumpet at the tables, long slaggy hair and black leather jackets, maxi skirts and boots like fishing waders. Maxine wasn't propping up the bar and picking at her stitches. The bloke running the auditions was a boxing promoter or the scrap man. He said I'd be second on after Dave there, and I could see straight off I'd ballsed it. The other blokes were already DJs, tight white jeans, sweatshirts which said: let's funk, gold nuggets round their necks. All of them had a little wooden brewery box full of singles. I should've stuck my head in my half o' lager and lime. Brown chords, tennis shoes, one of those tank-top jumpers from Chelsea Girl which only came down to an inch above my belly button, and a cloth cap. The grey velvet jacket over the top struck a contemporary note, but my sheepdog's hair and new second crop pubic beard made mockery of it. I had all my belongings in a hop sack, hastily packed, things to raise funds because I didn't have any money. I'd raised three quid from Mr Miles that morning but it was up in smoke already.

DJ Dave went on, really cocky. He made a voice like Scooby Doo and said the first girl to give him her knickers before the record ended won the pound note. I'd've taken my own knickers off for that quid if it'd counted. He hardly raised a titter. These were hard slags, their fags and lighters propped in front of them like tools of the trade, gin and limes, vodka and oranges. I think they'd been hired by the scrap man to intimidate us. No-one went for the pound. Dave signed off with more smart comments about coming back for the knickers after last orders, for which he got a few slow claps like he'd kicked over the dominoes.

Then a big shotgun finger pointed at me. I'd never spoken in public before. I said good evening like Alistair Cooke, but nothing happened. The microphone was switched off, I couldn't see the switch. It was too late to decide I'd confused this with a desire to announce programmes on the Home Service. There'd been an advert in Maxine's bloodied *Listener* for newsreaders in Scotland. That must've been the genuine 'green crow.' I'd chosen the black one, or the raven, in error. Well, at least I could apply for a newsreader job and say I'd been a DJ in London.

I looked at the boss, he came over, flicked the switch. I said testing, testing, one-two one-two. I sounded like the best man, unaccustomed as I was. Where're the records? I said. He said: Jesus, 'aven't you got none? No, I said and he pulled a box of singles out from under the turntables. I picked one out but couldn't read the label. There was a big hole in it. Good evenin', I said, again. Where were all those Radio Caroline/Top of The Pops catch-phrases? Hi-there, hop pickers... I looked out there but couldn't see them. The lights were dazzling, someone laughed. I thought I'd try Dave's patter instead, just to get going: well, uhm ladies' knickers, I didn't hear you... But they couldn't hear me, I was mumbling into my knickers. One of the slags shouted: play the fuckin' record, idiot. All right, I said. Here's a truly great sound, yeah, by ... by... I held the record up to the light. The Eagles. A really great sound from a really great group called The Eagles ... it's called *One of These Nights*... I lifted the arm and put the record on, then put the needle at the start. The turntable was static, this wasn't Neil Young in

130

the bedroom. I tried a switch and the other turntable came on. So I moved the record across. The needle swung over it making a scratch. I tried again, no sound, another switch, feedback. The volume was so deafening the boss slammed in and turned it down. It wasn't even *One of These Nights*; it must've been the flip side, *One of Those Days*. The girls were booing and laughing, the boss was at my ear: do us a favour, mate? I said sure. He said: fuck off home, do a jigsaw, don't come in 'ere again, all right?

I walked in circles looking for Chorley Crescent, to get my legs broken. I checked it again in the phone box. It was pissing down outside and I started to stink like a mouldy armchair. There was £1.27 in my pocket. My shoulders were cold and wet. I found a blue laundry bag with white plastic handles in a skip. Inside it was a raincoat, cotton on rubber, dark blue with one pearly button. I turned the collar up and stuffed my hair down inside, brushed off the plaster dust, transfered most of my tatt into the laundry bag. I really didn't know what to do. After sixty yards I pushed open a café door. Apart from the greaser at the jukebox it looked like a drop-in centre. There were two stale rolls and some cake crumbs under the glass counter. Cup of tea, packet of cheese and onion.

– You want sugar in it?

– How much is the cherry bun?

– Twelve pence. Do you want sugar or not?

Did Maxine take sugar in her tea? I couldn't remember, we rarely drank tea together. I had to keep her in mind because this city was crushing. Dark, foul air, my nails were already black, no one even looked at you.

– No, I said.

– You want that bun or not?

– No, just the crisps.

– Eighteen, please.

I stirred it anyway, just to buy time, but the plastic spoon snapped and the crisps were stale. I rolled a dog-end, smoked it to the stub, split it and emptied the over-sucked quidge into a tin. At the next table an old man with his hat on and the telly page in front of him dunked a Bourbon in his tea with one hand and marked with a biro what he was going to watch that night. A woman in a yellow tee-shirt with *body talk* written on her big tits was reading *Spare Rib*. The greaser played *The Green Manalishi* on the jukebox then sat down to scoff his corned beef and chips. The corned beef was the whole tinful.

– Cor, he said, this won't fly off the plate when someone opens the door, right?

The thing about these people, the thing that scared me: they didn't see you. It's as if you were watching telly and you could die in front of them, they wouldn't bother, but they'd expose themselves so publicly, relying on that mutual ignoring. Just getting the tube, Christ, I sat opposite this middle-aged couple. The bloke had a blue terylene suit worn shiny as a mirror, his nose and ears looked twisted on and half his teeth were silver. He spoke Polish to the woman, whose black hair was a girl's on a face like my gran's. She wore a white coat and queer white boots. The man had half the thumb missing from his left hand. He put his arm round the woman and began to rub her face with his stump. She kissed it and at one point took it into her mouth. Their knees were touching mine and it was like a threesome, an outrage, but to them it was nothing. Here you shared your life with ten million people. It was London. And supposing Maxine, once there – if she was there – became the same conditioned being, hardened to put up with the filth and the rush. She wouldn't notice me. I felt invisible. They all had lives, but the lives were slots, they fitted into back-alleys and tiny blackened windows that rattled like greaseproof paper and were never opened. They lived with deafening noise. Everything cost so much. How could a London Maxine be the same Maxine I'd known? This was what scared me. I'd got it all so wrong. It wasn't Plato Villa here. She took decisions in her life I could never understand. I saw what she meant when she said she hated London. I wouldn't have coped in a place like that. What could I possibly say to shake her world upside down?

I needed somewhere to sleep now. I found these streets and squares of guest houses and seedy hotels down both sides of the pavement. *Vacancies,* it said on every door and window, strip-lights, dull bulbs, warped curtains, glimpses of striped pink wallpaper, sagging net curtains with their catch of flies, yellow smoke, a shadow of a guest, the black and white flickers of a telly. I walked up and down bent into the wind one way, or let it sweep me down the street like a crisp packet the other. I was starving, knackered, broke. My scalp itched, I stank, my smoking finger was a yellowing crust. That was what London had done in less than six hours. The nearer I got to Maxine, the more I disintegrated. She might've been a glimpse across the street away. She could've passed me a million times that day and neither of us would've known.

The Aurora looked the most like a doss-house. Porch light swinging unfixed to its rose, flickering for a blow. In a basement passage a dustbin lid rolled clanking in imperfect circles. The black iron handrail rusted into my hand. Reception, green carpets, green walls, a keyboard full of keys to empty rooms. Someone walking on the floor above, rooms 1-20 to the left beside a fire extinguisher. The night porter's office was locked. Someone was watching a telly in the lounge off the passage. A door I hadn't seen opened and a skinny bloke about my age stood looking at me. Porter's cap, silver shades and a tee-shirt under his jacket. He looked surprised. He looked like I shouldn't be there, like he'd just mopped the floor. I pushed the laundry bag up against the counter with my feet. A note scrawled in pencil said: back in a mo. The porter disappeared again. A blonde girl with a round face and dry cracked lips came back.

– You the guest? she said.
– Yes. I'd like a room.
– Single?
– Yes.
– Not with them comfrence, are yer?
She cackled like Auntie Beryl. Too young to cackle like that.
– No.
– 'Ow long for?
– Uhm, two nights.
She flicked through the register and scribbled with her pencil, biting her lip.
– Six parnd eighty an' a parnd for the key, please.
The cheeks under my eyes were quivering now. I couldn't think of anything to say. The only thing in my head was: 27 Chorley Crescent.
– Uhm, you want the money now? I said.
– Yes please.
The porter was hovering to my right, screwing my laundry bag.
– I can't go to the bank till morning, I said. Is that all right?
– Not really, she said. How do we know you won't run off

without paying?

The porter was laughing now, sort of panel-beating giggle. I took my laundry bag with my last few pence of dignity and left. I was thirty yards down the street when the porter shouted 'fucking prat' after me. And now my shoelace snapped as I tried to re-tie it and my socks kept slipping down under my heels.

The Peak Hotel was locked. There was a bell I didn't feel like ringing. Before I had a chance to retreat, some bloke opened up and gave me room twenty, a quid deposit for the key. That left me with 9p and they didn't do food, cup of tea if I was lucky, the bloke said, the quid returned when I settled up. My room was school-green too, no bigger than the bed. There was a washbasin to piss in, a bedside cabinet with a hair-clip in it, a black phone with no dialler, like a shop dummy without a crack between its legs. As I drew the curtain I noticed it was two floors up with no drainpipe to shin down, no balcony or fire-escape. Spotlights ghost-wrote for the moon in the yard. Unless there was a window on the landing I'd have to go out the front door and run for it. I'd signed the register as H. Pollenfex, c/o Oxford University. With my last 9p I went out and bought the most I could get for it, a packet of chocolate-covered Garibaldi biscuits and a packet of Rizlas. I split my bag of dog-ends and rolled twenty straights, all packed into a DuMaurier box I'd found on the train. My belly was tight from its Garibaldi stuffing, three left for the morning. In my bag I'd got some socks and pants, a shirt, another pair of trousers, but mostly stuff to flog, heirlooms saved from old Steptoe's grasp, my old man's watch, brass letter-opener, leather wallet, electric shaver, Parker Pen. I slipped into the nylon sheets with my pants on in case I had a wet dream. Second-hand fag, Kingsley Amis novel, picking and fiddling under the sheets, waiting for sleep to deaden the next day's advance.

twenty-two

Half-past eight that cripple of a phone rang. The bastard downstairs wanted me to pay by 9.30 or get out while he still had egg between his teeth. Didn't even ask me if I'd slept well or had a nice wet dream, nor offer me that cup of tea. I slapped some water round my stale regions and put the soap and towel in my bag. On my way along the corridor I remembered the mirrors on the staircase, someone at the bottom could see me coming down, in 3-D probably. There were no windows, or none that didn't plunge thirty feet into the basement or the cellar steps. The courtyards were landbound, dustbin alleys, slippery yellow bricks, places where idiots went to get murdered in detective films. So I tiptoed down into reception, ready to leg it into the crowd scene. The receptionist was drinking my cup of tea and reading a newspaper. Someone was hoovering. There was dusty sunlight on the window stickers. I kept my laundry bag low and put the keys on the desk. She looked up, I said 'morning,' grabbed the door and was gone. Turned the first corner and jogged, looked back at the second corner but I was safe.

I was walking through Portobello Market looking for Chorley Crescent when I saw the pawnbrokers half-hidden by a fabric stall. A woman in dairy boots was flicking at dogs with her tape measure. A blue arrow pointed up a narrow flight of stairs. The fruit and veg market was up this end too and there was stuff in the gutter, a nice apple, a big tomato. I bent for the apple but this foot wellied it aside. I stood to see whose red welly, and the apple was tossed into a baby's pram.

– It's a rat-race, mate, the bloke said.

He was my age, sheepskin coat over a pyjama jacket, blue cords tied with string, face as white as his pram, buck teeth, thin curls on top and a mop each side of his head. I'd never seen such a ponce. He turned his pram round and pulled it backwards to stand right in my face. I looked in the pram. It was full of mungo. All the chrome was ripped away, rusty holes, the shreds of hood hanging down both sides. The bloke looked like his pram. Apart from my apple he had some leaves, a fridge hinge, a sheet of jagged metal with the green paint blistered, a roller skate with a missing wheel and a porno mag with the cover torn off.

– John, listen, he said. Wanna do a deal?

– What kind of deal?

– Know where Chorley Crescent is?

– What about it?

– Well, John, see this?

He pulled a key out from the top slit of his sheepskin.

– What about it?

– Don't talk to me like that, John, I'm criminel de panache, man. They've heard of me in the arse of beyond. This is the fuckin' key to your dreams. House full of bigguns, no-one ever in, I'll even tell yer where to sell the stuff after.

– What stuff ?

– Fuckin' Nora, just give me a fiver for the key then go find out yerself.

– What number Chorley Crescent?

– Ah, yer don't catch me with that one, John.

– It's twenny-seven, isn't it?

– Might be.

– I don't have a fiver.

– Whatcher got, then?

– Nothing.

– What, not even a squid?

– I'm skint.

– Where d'yer live?

– I've nowhere to sleep, if that's what yer mean.

– Yeah, that is what I mean. You better sort yourself out, John, 'cause when you see me sitting in a restaurant with a plate of chips you'll feel sick being the bloke who turned down the best deal in London. Just remember who offered it to yer.

– Look, I'll get you a quid for the key if you swear it's twenny-seven.

– I fuckin' swear, on me 'onour, John, it's twenny-seven. What yer gonna do for the quid? Hail Mary?

– Pawnshop.

– You'll be lucky. 'E wouldn't give yerra quid fer the Crown

Jewels.

There was a whole list on the glass door. Solicitor, dentist, private detective, marriage guidance. That made it four out of five for Maxine to come in, apart from the custard yellow walls, the musty waff. I was fifth in the queue at the grill. The couple at the front had a colour telly they'd dragged up the stairs. They wanted £150. The pawnbroker offered twenty. They said it was worth £300.

– I don't usually take televisions.

The woman said:

– Let's just sell it, Jed. We can rent one, it doesn't matter.

– Twenty pounds, take it or leave it. Please, there's people waiting.

– Stuff it mate, the bloke said.

They shoved past with the great telly in their arms. The bloke said to me:

– I wouldn't wait 'ere, mate, not to see that bloody miser.

I heard the plug bumping down the stairs behind them. The woman in front of me had a box of rings. She took two out and tried leaning into the grill so you couldn't hear what she said. There were two sets of curlers behind me started talking soon as the plug stopped bumping.

– You've got a couple like that, aincha? On your block? Well, I 'ad a jade Gothic cross, forty years. Me 'usband, whose fucked off now didn't yer know, 'e 'ad it made for me before we was married. That woman picked it up when I dropped it, didn't dawn on me at the time. Gothic art it were. Said she'd lost it! Always call 'er a thief when I see 'er. THIEF, she shouted back down the stairs.

That made the pawnbroker glare. He screwed his eye into a glass and looked at the rings breathing hard through his nose.

– Six, he said.

– Is that all, six pounds each?

– Not each, six pounds for both.

– But they're diamonds.

– No they're not. They're glass.

– What about this, then?

She shoved her hand through the grill.

– It's my engagement ring. That's diamonds I know.

– Take it off, let me see it properly … All right, it's a diamond, a cheap one. Six-fifty. Twelve-fifty all three.

He shoved all mine back at me. Shaver, pen, watch, lighter. He shook his head.

– I'm not a charity shop.

– But it's a Parker Pen.

– So what.

– The watch is waterproof.

– So am I.

– It's a good watch. My old man was very particular about his watches. Date, shockproof.

– I'm shockproof too. One pound five pence the watch, take the rest away.

Mungo Jerry still had the key and held my quid up to the light, snapping it a few times.

– Boneo, he said. One key to paradise. Don't be a piss-kitchen John and use it now, will yer. Wait till later, just don't go thinking yer penny's silver all of a sudden. See yer later…

Soon as I had the key it unlocked the logic. That quid was two days dinner down the spout. Or the deposit for a night's kip. Even if it was the key to Maxine's door, what good would it do me? I didn't want to nick her telly or smell her perfumed knickers. If she was there, I'd wait outside, maybe follow her, and when she stopped for a cup of coffee I'd choose my moment and slip into the vacant chair … So why had I sacrificed my old man's watch and spent the quid on a bent key some loony found in the gutter? I kidded myself that it was to protect Maxine, or her property, from someone else breaking in. Pity she couldn't know I'd do this for her instead of smearing shit round her kitchen, pissing in her fridge, shoving the void back up her arse. Society had its force-field working that day.

I was starving hungry too, my stomach shrinking in a wash of digestive juices. Just a cup of tea, for chrissake. Five pence and a pawn ticket, as broke as the sky at dawn. I looked at the ticket. Half a pence on the pound every first month, five pence on the pound excess on the first month per article per pound. Pawnbroker sells the article after two years if unclaimed.

27, Chorley Crescent from a safe distance had no distinguishing tremors. Just a brick look-alike in Victorian London. There was no maroon Maxi parked outside, no dark car like the one I saw at Plato Villa. I felt no great emotion coming here either, just a further sinking, like the onset of hyperthermia, or an innocent prisoner on the first day of a life sentence. You'd better start studying the law or you're gonna die in your cell. And short of killing Maxine, nothing I could do right then would make a difference. I still rang the number from the phone box on the corner, watching her front door. There was no answer, and no-one came or went. I let the phone ring and ring, as if it was a probe I'd sent into space, my satellite going from room to room until it formed a shape, my outline, my hands, my heart. And it sank onto her bed and slept. I was crying as I put the phone down. They hadn't even waited in to see if I'd come. I wasn't worth worrying about. Gerald didn't even want to break my legs.

I walked up the brick steps. The front door was black with brass numbers. The bell was like dropping a stone down a dry well. Right, I was going in. I would smear shit on their walls and thumb through Maxine's knickers. I might even find some cash. Or the safe where she kept the avocados and the poems her other 'contributors' sent in. The key, that poxy key, it wouldn't even fit in the lock, the ponce. I threw it down the basement steps and hammered on the door.

   – You tosser, Gerald. Come out here and break my legs!

twenty-three

Small Mercy left me a note on our respective third week in separate pads. Cheap biro free with every coffin, gouging through the letter pad. Be here when I go, it said, as if it was a suicide note, not a summons. Three weeks of living alone and both of us wanted to go elsewhere.

I set off through the village towards Kilner Road. As I cut past the old fire station I found myself behind Mrs Tugwell, our ex-neighbour. I waited till she'd turned the corner and gone. Didn't want her asking how life was treating me, now I'd left me poor old Mum. Last time she saw me she'd said: when yer gonna tie the knot, Enry? She probably meant the one round my neck, come to think of it.

Outside the bungalow, cousin Ricky's white Pontiac took up half the pavement. They cost wages, a year of time and a half, and now the payments. We'd heard all about that at the funeral. So, they'd come to take Small Mercy away for a bit, help her through the worst, as none of it was getting better. Auntie Beryl blocked the kitchen door as I opened it.

– Coo look oo it ain't, Mercy. All right then, are we, Enry?

Aunty Beryl painted her lips post-office red, thick as planks, inflatable smiles liable to peel off in shrieks of laughter. She was the youngest by ten years of the seven sisters, an Avon Lady. Small Mercy was Yardley so it was like a stink fixture, the perfume derby. Beryl was the biggest and the loudest too, bright yellow skirts in the middle of winter, green high heels, big white handbags bulging from dozens of houseparties. She'd thrown Uncle Nobby out, the Brylcreme squirt with a shiney little tache, and he was living in a caravan down the bottom of Beryl's back garden in Essex with some girl half his age.

– Settled in yer noo place, 'ave we, Enry? she said. Ricky's in the front room. Go say 'ello. Doan offen see yer now, do we. Funerals and weddings, ain'it.

Ricky mumbled when he saw me:

140

– Whatcheer, moosh.

He was smoking a Long Thin rolled in liquorice paper. His dog-blonde hair moulting round a bald saucer, bum-fluff like it was stuck on flypaper. He was only twenty-one. His bored girlfriend rubbed her bare legs under the table, prizing her shoes off with raw toes.

– Doan mind Della, Ricky said. She juss give up smokin' dope fer the noo year, the manky cow.

– Sharrup you.

Ricky was divorced at nineteen. His ex-wife used to eat jam straight out the jar. The baggots took me round there one Sunday afternoon, not far from Beryl's in Stanford-le-Hope. A rented bungalow, cracked patio full of weeds and dog ends, the front room smelt like a pub. Stained carpets, party kegs of shipwreck bitter rolling round the floor, Genesis albums clogging up the sofa. The idea was to leave me there while the grown-ups went off for a natter:

– Doan do nuffin' we wouldn't do, Beryl said.

I stared at the piled ashtrays while Ricky twanged his guitar and fatty stuffed her face with jam. When I looked in their aquarium Ricky said:

– That's Ghengis, me pirhana. Likes 'is jam, dun'e. Finks it's yuman flesh.

Then he'd dropped his voice to a whisper:

– 'Ere, Enry me ol' cuz, wanna eat some dope cake wiv me an' Sue artside?

We ate the lot, then started on the Scotch. Ricky spiked my drink and I was spewing up all the way home and the baggots said they were never taking me in the car with them again.

Nothing had changed. Ricky was balder, maybe, and his new bird looked like she'd got jam round her eyes.

– How's work? I said, looking at the Pontiac. Paid it off yet?

We'd gone through all that at the funeral too. Ricky still had the same job. Mortician, Brentwood General.

– Same as ever, Ricky said. Bit dead, hahahaha.

Aunty Beryl came in and Small Mercy flushed the toilet, coming out pulling her skirt down at the hem.

– 'Ello boy. Saw you 's mornin comin' art Watsons. Whatyer buyin' down there then? Ge'n yer old ma a corset? I toldyer I'd get yer undypants meself nex' time I wen' in Marks, if I live long

141

enough to go t'Tumbridge Wells, that is. Well?

– Well what?

– What y'after down Watsons?

I was after a new cloth cap and a pair of Doc Martens, but I wasn't telling her that.

– A belt, if yer must know.

– A belt? Heavens boy, a belt me foot! Yer should've had one o' yer father's belts. Old Miles prob'ly still has 'em. You wanna put some weight on yer, 'ave yer mills round 'ere, then yer wouldn't need one. You used t'like my cooking.

– I don't live 'ere any more.

I was upset then, she'd made me drop an 'h' and say 'ere. Since college I'd disguised the twang. I'd made her sarcastic too.

– Nah, I don't s'pose you do, if that's what yer call livin'. Dossin' in ole Steptoe's rotten attic. Caw, if you knoo'd lived up there down the years.

– Christ, I've hardly unpacked yet. You've never seen in there, anyway.

– No, an' I doan aff to neether. I know what goes on.

She poured five teas in the kitchen.

– Still like yawn this colour, don't yer boy? Or that changed an' all?

The bungalow was spick and span already, even jaded. As if she'd been there years. It was polished daily, perpetual scrutiny, but more to rid it of Miss Roach than contemporary scum. The atmosphere from no. 51 had been reproduced, as if she'd hoovered it up, vacuumed it, kept it in the fridge, carried it up there in freezer bags and spread it out around her. Instead of family photographs there were those walls of ice where our past life inside them was a frozen blur for all to see. She didn't look any different to before. She was always the pre-widow with the short grey hair in the monthly perm who'd begun to look like Nan. Her life was no more isolated in the bungalow than when her George was alive to keep the ice walls blast frozen. Was she intending to keep up the chronic outbursts? Had she packed all the pent up bitterness and carted that up the bungalow too? If she had, then did it mean he wasn't the cause after all?

Thinking like that made me hunger for the words again. The words I needed for my rage against Maxine. It suprised me that, discovering that love was also a rage. I wanted to put the two of them in the same room again, Maxine and Small Mercy. If she could drag up that bitterness we'd have had a hen fight, Maxine shredded by cares she never knew existed. It would be more effective than anything I could say, unless I found the means, those words that didn't yet exist. Small Mercy's shit-poor life was the poem I couldn't write. Sometimes I could've wept for her in genuine something-or-other. Life and death with him had amputated her from family. But at least there'd been a them, an each other, a Mr & Mrs on the envelopes, a Mum 'n Dad on the birthday cards, a Dad on the wreath, a Son in the 'left behind' column. She'd been left with nothing though, not a thing in the world, so wouldn't that be worth an outburst? Shouldn't she have been howling in the house against that bit of the Almighty's arithmetic homework? Was my rage hers after all?

– Go on, boy, she said, blowing her tea cold. Why don't yer come with us to Stamford lee 'Ope? Whatyer gonna do, fer heaven's sake, si'n all on yer own?

– I've told you. I've got things to do.

– Well, fancy wantin' to stay all on yer todd.

Ricky was smirking at us over his weak, sweet tea, kicking Della under the table like: told yer so, watch this:

– All shacked up with that fancy woman, inch 'Enry mate?

– Doan be s'crude, Ricky, Small Mercy said. That's all finished, you 'ear? Finished!

She was packing me some things in carrier bags. Aunty Beryl was on the bog now, humming loudly and running the taps while bombing Dresden and China.

– Nah, Ricky said to me, don't worry cuzz. Come over fer nex Christmas. I gotta work Boxin' Day meself. Boxin' up the leftovers, hahahaha. Lotsa stiffs come in that time o' year. All them stiff drinks, hahaha, get it, Del? Nah listen, I've got me work keys 'ere look – skeleton keys, hahahaha. Still, not a bad job, is it, Del? Nice little urner, boom-boom…

– Show some respect, yer whippersnapper, Small Mercy said. Yer uncle still fresh in his grave… Well then? Come 'ere, boy. Now, 'ere's some cake, some nuts, look, in this bag. Yer doan like Fig Rolls, do yer…

All the Christmas leftovers for my new life.

– Cor, I wouldn't mind a good fig, Aunty Mercy, Ricky shouted.

– Figs don't grow on trees, yer know, Ricky. Look, Henry! Concentrate. Now, keep this on top. I've put it in clingfilm so it won't slip down. An' this is from Beryl'n Ricky, yer Christmas present what she's kept back for yer.

Aunty Beryl came out the bog, fresh coat of lipstick like she'd just taken it still wet off the peg, so sheeny it caught the lightbulb. We all reached for the gas masks too.

– Oh it's nothing much, Mercy. I expect 'e's got plenty already.

– What, got 'im some brains then, Mum? Ricky said.

– Pay attention Henry, please. You're like a flippertygibbet. There's a few bits 'n pieces in this Tupperware. I wan 'em back, mind. Yer needn't wash 'm. Well? Whadda yer say, then?

– Thank you.

Ricky was stretching and yawning. Aunty Beryl said:

– Cor, look at rubberman.

twenty-four

The West Kent Branch of the Schools Action Union was defunct now, but I'd still got a satchel full of leaflets. I couldn't think of a better ruse for hanging about the walled cloisters of Gunmakers School, where generations of Pollenfex majors and minimuses had learnt their cricket, classics and cadet drill. I'd be a voice from the dead, too, because the head, known as The Dungeon, Mr Bartlett Dunne-Johns MA (Cantab), was institutional in the SAU's demise. Demise wasn't the word, really: we fell apart in the Ego-Trip Wars. Bad rift with the T. Wells branch of the White Panthers started it, during a joint jumble sale. They hadn't wanted Peter Hain from the Students Union to come and open it, saying he was a Maoist. Hain refused to come down anyway, saying the SAU were the Maoists. The Panthers helped themselves to the macrobiotic food before the fucking doors were open, then when they released the fire-bars at ten sharp to let the old biddies in, one of them had shouted 'No rip-offs.' The feud was on, each accusing the other of being in politics for the ego-trip. The SAU were all West Kent College bourgeois who thought the proleteriat lived in cute poverty with home-made bread in our larders. Accusing us of rip-offs was patronising. The White Panthers, now defunct themselves, were radical freedom fighters who believed in firing squads but only operated between their parents' town houses and the saloon bar of The Sussex where, as they worshipped their Newcastle Brown, all they talked about was Lindisfarne and Trotsky. But The Dungeon had done for us by ganging together with other grammar heads and bombing our college with complaints that we'd been leafleting their pupils with seditious propoganda. College threatened to expel us, the pubs banned our meetings, even the pigs turned up once. Apathy stepped in to save us.

Gunmakers was a Gothic bodge of red brick and butresses with a spire in the middle, coming off the roof. Known as the arms dealers' school, because it was an arm of the Woshipful Society of Gunmakers. Old Gunners made good tank commanders or made their mark in Varsity rugger before distinguished careers in the Foreign Office or the Gaurds or selling rocket launchers to schizophrenic dictators. Gerald's background, according to Maxine. Her old man had got Gerald into the Stock Exchange after the Guards, and there's not much she could've done about it.

Quarter to four seemed like a good time to assemble in Gunmakers Passage. Tunbridge Wells just erupted with moulten pupils, reducing the average age of pedestrians by tenfold, and swelling the population by the power of a hundred. But just to enhance my anonymity, I'd put the glad-rags on. Grey velvet jacket, the herring-bone flares, new desert boots I got with another clothing allowance, green shirt with the butterfly collar. The pocket-watch was a neat touch, a fleck of toff to put the chaps, the 'small arms' as they'd been known in the SAU, at ease. Trouble was, Gunmakers by decree was a hair-above-the-collar school, and mine was a bit progressive.

The day-boys' eyes were in their nostrils as they came out in sporadic fire, then a sudden hail. I tried politeness. Excuse me please… I kept saying. All I wanted to do was ask if anyone knew James and Piers Pollenfex-O'Connor. I didn't expect the day boys to be so harsh. 'Ooh, ducky' and 'get a haircut, The Dungeon's coming.' So I resorted to the leaflets. Snatch and drop, and there were leaflets all over the fucking place so I went round picking them up as if they were pound notes. One little cunt kicked me up the arse. I went nearer the school gates where behaviour might still be bound by surveillence. I should've asked after Pollenfex first, because the leaflets were balled back, half-pint tadpole Guards just flicking them in my face. Then the elite did a walk past, the Eton subs bench, single-file to throw the balled-up leaflets back, also in my face. 'Scum,' they said, each one to a man. Jesus, what race are they? Three prefects on duty, watching the fun, now strolled across with set jaws as if there was an invisible strap holding the regimental cap in place.

– What's going on here? one of them snapped, as if he was auditioning for *Flashman Joins the Gestapo*.

And like the snivelling prol I was, what did I do? My fisted salute stayed up my sleeve. All slogans retracted and back in the bag and the revolutionary sunrise was blotted out. Flashman made a grab and all three held a conflab over the leaflet. I should've run for it.

Instead, I was cranking out the faux-posh and saying:

– Axshully, chaps, that's not why I'm really here, you know. I was rather hoping to have a word with one of your boarders. I've a ... uhm, a letter from his mother, you know ...

– This rubbish says you're from the Schools Action Union. I thought The Dungeon put the blockers on you scum.

And before I could say 'oh damn, I thought they were Boy Tory handouts,' they had me in an arm-lock they must have learned in Cadets that morning.

– Great work, Flashman said. He's immobilized. I'll get The Dungeon. Still in school house, yah?

– You're making a terrible mistake, I said.

– No we're not, scum.

They weren't, were they. They were sniffer dogs. They were fucking x-ray kids and they could see right into your baked bean soul. In their drilled and geiger-counting world I stuck out like a contaminated thumb. Sub-strata, under-wanker. I was on the flip-side where you flunked the eleven-plus and went to Swattenden Rural County Secondary Modern for Scumboys and your stink stayed with you for life. Even the tekkies said Swattenden was Borstal, and most of us agreed with them. An ugly eighteenth-century country house, whitewashed grey and window-taxed blank, surrounded by post-war Ministry of Education huts. Pigsties and gardening masters and C Streams which flowed into Swattenden from natural springs bringing a flood of village idiots from Sandhurst, Hawkhurst, Cranbrook, Sissinghurst, Frittenden, Benenden, Goudhurst and Staplehurst.

After Raynor slung me out I was allowed back just for the prize-giving. The riot-like euphoria among the leavers as we boys poured into the future, pissing up Raynor's office door as we went, smashing up DD's car and shouting 'fuck off Millsy-pillsy.' If we'd been educated at all we might at least have called him Satanic Mills as we searched and destroyed. We'd sung the school hymn for the last time: *Soldiers of Christ arise and put your armour on* ... And that was it: good luck, boys, your schooldays are over.

There was a chasm in society that no book-reading would ever fill. Those inheritors of the earth really scared me too, in their purple caps, braided blazers with Latin tags scrolled across the pockets, brown leather shoes, American raincoats, cravats. Swattenden

147

boys'd worn second-hand blazers two sizes too big, missing buttons, elbows hanging out of pullovers, wet smelly plimsolls in the snow. Hards wore winkle-pickers with the uppers snapping open from the sole like gaping pike jaws gripping their mangled prey of blue toes. Swattenden ploggers, scuffing moochers, farm animals. Sly, dim, banana-backed, we slung hangjaw into class or stomped provocatively into shops making a vicious face at anything in our path. We were bottle-kickers, rubber-chuckers, phlobber deluxes.

– What the hell are you up to?

The Dungeon was pointing his finger at me.

I didn't know what I was up to, did I. I'd just wanted to see them, these boys whose future Maxine said I'd complicated. The family unit she'd dumped me for.

– Let him go, DeVille, Fox, and well done.

– Perhaps I should explain, sir, I said.

– Perhaps you'd better. I thought I'd put a stop to this subversive tomfoolery. You and your damned rebel-rousers.

– Yes, yes, that was a mistake, I'm sorry. The SAU don't exist any more. The thing is, I have a message, a letter, for one of your boys.

– Who?

– Pollenfex. Uh, the older one.

– That's Piers. What's your connection with him, exactly?

– I'm a friend of his mother's.

– Then why couldn't she have contacted him through the usual channels? I don't like the smell of this one bit.

– She's, uhm, may I talk to you alone, in confidence?

– No you may not. This is all highly irregular. I'm inclined to call the police.

We were mobbed by boys now, all peering at the captured beast, a weird wheeze on the quad.

– I'm not speaking in front of all these boys, I said.

The Dungeon hadn't noticed. He put his spectacles on and peered round about.

– Private scrum, boys; run along now.

When they'd dispersed, I said:

– It's rather delicate, you see. She's uhm, she's ill, again.

– Oh, I see. All right. But I'm not sure this is the way to go about things. DeVille, run and find Pollenfex-O'Connor Maximus. He'll be in Moseley House. I don't like this one bit.

Not a word passed their lips as we waited. I think they wanted me to leg it, revert to type, save us all the trouble of social travesty, great embarrassment. For me just any brief moment of equality was worth it, I'd sunk so low. False or not. I hated myself for it, and hated them for it too. One slip of acceptance, one flicker of doubt that they might have misjudged me, on their faces, signed in flesh, was all I'd wanted. And what faces. The Dungeon square as a soggy book, crumpling the further down it went, pulling his mouth into a pained sneer. His jacket was half blazer, club buttons, secret society, I don't know. He was probably just another Baptist Church organist at heart. If only I could loathe them and not care if they felt the same about me. That was probably the only way. Loathe the whole family, Maxine most of all.

The boys, the young gentlemen, stood 'at ease,' basking in the ring of authority. Master Fox had long thin fingers which curled backwards. They even had freckles on them. When he looked at me during one lighthouse like sweep of his head on the world, he pursed his lips and blew me a kiss, the most repulsive act of hatred I'd ever seen. The other, Flashman, set his tongue chasing round his teeth for a strand of roast pheasant, keeping his jaw on a left slant the entire time, the face of an Englishman on the field of honour. He snapped to attention.

– Here they come, sir.

Piers Pollenfex, the boy who could have been, in my vision of how things should have gone, my fourteen-year-old stepson. Had Maxine made him like she made a poem? Had he been cut from her with a bread-knife? Was she fucked like the moon to produce this star, this exploding planet, or was he the debris, doomed like her to orbit a useless, lifeless space? I looked at him as if he was Maxine, the way he held his arms behind his back to hide the scars, the eyes which held residues of sleepless nights, the lips which still kissed me in the dark when I wasn't there.

– Do you know this person? The Dungeon asked him.

– No sir, Piers said.

In his effort to face me he extinguished Maxine's features with a scowl, a mask of unknown boy, a portcullis of spite.

– He says, Piers, that he's come from your mother, with a message.

– I don't think so, sir.

– He's been coaxed, I said.

– Don't be absurd, The Dungeon said.

– Then how could he know?

– That's enough. I'm bringing this farce to an end. I'm sorry I put you through this, Piers, this painful masquarade. Run along now, you can speak to me later if you like, and not a word to James, eh?

– No sir, thank you, sir.

He was a boy again, Maxine's face when free of me, returning to his school for the sake of tradition, the uncomplicated advance of generations who, when a wild thing like Maxine broke the pledge, turned on her to stamp her out, made her cut herself, staunch her poetry, threaten to take her children away.

– PIERS, I DO KNOW YOUR MOTHER. I LOVED HER, SHE LOVED ME. DON'T LET THEM...

And he came towards me with his fists out, face convulsed. It was her face now, even his hair was dark auburn and matched the locks I'd got in my shrine, and for a second we were in the same blood-red world together, the free-Maxine world before the lithium eyes and the copelessness. He screamed at me, and it was the voice of Gerald, and the way was cleared. The drill-hall way, the rugger field, the Guards, mother was neurotic, she had to be sent away...

– Don't talk about my mother. Leave her alone! She doesn't know you! She wouldn't love you, scrotum!

Yeah, well, I knew, in my heart of hearts, I knew he was right. He spoke for all the Pollenfexes in the world. It was up to me to speak back, for all the Chambers on the planet.

twenty-five

It was late April, all the hedgerows luminous green and a bitter wind slashed through the fruit trees to scatter blossom in the fields. A cuckoo echoed all day long over Little Switzerland. Some of the drab down Kilner Road had washed away in a splatter of daffodil and tulip. Small Mercy was smoking her first fag of the day, oblivious to Spring. The hoover was freshly coiled away in the shoe cupboard, the dusters shaken, the smell of wax polish humming on the few items of furniture. She sat on a mended armchair wearing a silver green, transparently thin cardigan. The place was freezing. The monthly perm was due; she sat stiff as a broom handle waiting out for my footsteps, dropping saccharin tabs in her tea. The spoon was a souvenir of somewhere she'd never been. I knocked on the back door, opened it myself and shouted:

– 'S oany me.

She didn't move.

– Wiped yer feet?

Halfway through the kitchen I said yes-yes.

– So it's you then, is it? she said.

I stood in the doorway to be looked over, knowing she knew.

– D'ya wanna cuppa tea then, or not? Yer c'n put the water on too. I shall wan' another.

I took my cup in and sat at the table.

– Why don't yer sit down 'ere where I can see yer, boy?

I moved to the armchair.

– What's that cup y've got there? What's wrong with yer usual cup? Not good enough for y'all of a sudden?

– Fancied a change, that's all.

– Oh yeah? Pull the other one! Now what's goin' on! Where've yer bin, any'ow? Yer never come t'see yer ol' ma these days. That bloomin' woman still, in'it. Still givin' yer the runaround, ain't she?

There was nothing I could say she'd believe. I looked out the window. I could see Wayne's mum who lived just over the road. She always hung her washing in the front garden. I could see Wayne's Suzuki by the dustbin.

– What woman's that, then?

– God Almighty's cow, boy, oo d'yer think. You leave this village and you'll be back 'ere in a Black Maria.

– Who told you I was leaving!

– Who d'yer think! Blabber-mouth in the bloomin' fag shop. 'E 'eard it from that bloody Steptoe Miles, never could keep his box shut. Fancy chuckin' in a roof over yer 'ead. You ain' even gotta sleepin' bag since the Police used the last one in evidence against yer!

– Keep yer hair on. My probation's over. I'm goin' to live with a friend, out Ashford way.

– You ain' got no frenz.

– Oh yes I have. I'm gonna share a house with Bill Davis, see. He's got a job designing album covers for Van de Graaf Generator … Said I can help him … write the words …

That must've been one of the crappiest lies I'd ever told. And I'd said I was going to see Bill Davis the night I did the pharmacy, too. He'd come looking for me once, had Bill, that summer. Walked from Benenden with some ricket- looking kid half his age. Bill had orange-glo loons and a purple skullcap, sideboards like fuckin' ginger haybales. Said he was walking about Southern England trying to score some acid. Did I have any? Did I know where he could get any? When I said, are you still playing for Arsenal, he said no, I'm designing album covers for Van de Graaf Generator.

– There's the ke'l boilin', Small Mercy said. Go an' see to it.

I put my cup down and went to stand up.

– Oh, never mind, jack-ape, I'll do it. You're too slow.

She always did that. And I always stared at the patterns on the brown hearth tiles, tracing their shapes with my tongue round the back of my teeth, the same tiles as down the other house.

– Well?

She wasn't giving up.

– Well what?

– When yer leavin'?

She wiggled in her chair, Lady Dignity sipping tea and blowing smoke like a beginner.

– Tomorrow.

– Well, boy, yer managed to kill yer father and Pinky, s'now it's my turn, is it? What did we ever do to you!

– Oh, fer fuck's sake. I'm goin'...

– Wash yer mouth out, boy, and talk proply t'yer mother!

The mantle clock pendulum like dripping water in a bucket. Instant depression, time just leaking away. Get out while there's time.

– You still 'aven't told me a thing. If you're goin' after that floozy then all I can say is good riddance to yer.

Banana-backed in the armchair, I threw out the first flippant quip I could think of.

– Yeah, we're getting married, if you must know.

I thought it would shut her up, that's all.

– Fibber. You always was a fibber. Should be ashamed of 'erself, then. You an' all, be all accounts. 'Ow can yer show yerself up like this after all I bin through? You should marry yer own kind.

– Oh, what, like some of them twats you an' Dad used to worship, them snobs we put our Sunday best on for...

– You keep that evil mouth o' yawn shut, d'you 'ear! You'll 'ave yer poor father turnin' in 'is blinkin' grave.

She snapped shut like her purse on milk day, emptied the ashtray in the wastebin, singing:

I doan know whyyyyyyyyyyyyyyyyyyyy
There's no sun-up in the skyyyyyyyyy
Stawmy wea-therrrrrrrrrrr...

I danced round the room like a puppet whose strings just fell off.

– You fuckin' martyr. Look what he did to us. Too ashamed to be alive.

The singing stopped, as if I'd unplugged her vacuum cleaner.

– You get out of here ... and doan' come back till I'm dead and gone.

I stamped my way to the back door and wrenched it open. The peg bag spilled on the floor. She twisted her hanky round her little finger and dabbed at tear-gas eyes, two chipped marbles tucked into red gashes.

– I watched yer father make a fool of 'imself fer years an' you think I doan' understand? Just mark my words, stay where yer belong. Now then, pick them pegs up before yer go.

Next morning I packed a rucksack with some clothes and grub. Everything not already up Small Mercy's just went down the coal-hole into the second-hand bargain basement. My mind was like an unlatched door banging in the wind. From the window I watched people walk from shop to shop.

Small Mercy came out of the baker's. She tensed outside the tobacconist's, pulling at her skirt, bracing her shoulders. Proud-up, hauty flutter of her arse before flushing Dennis's bog-handled door, crossing his threshold like a kitchen slut turning up to boil the semolina.

I didn't have to hear it to know how it went. He'd always described to me what he called 'anuvver brush with Ena Sharples.' Dennis was mending watches in the back. He came out with an eye-glass stuck in a squint. He popped it into his hand like a joke eye, smirking when he saw who it was.

– Mornin', Missus.

She was sharp:

– Whassa matter with you?

– Nothin' much, thank you. Usual, is it? Or does your Enry want hahaha four ounce o' shag today?

– O' course usual. Whatya think I am, made o' money?

– Oany askin', like. Juss bein' yer friendly shopkeeper, hold yer wig on. I see old burgler Bill's packed 'is bags, then. Jumped 'is probation, 'as 'e?

Every week she'd bought ten Kensitas tipped for herself and a half ounce of Old Holborn for me. She slipped it through my letterbox, thinking I never saw her coming. Dennis put them on the counter and leaned across.

– 'Ere, cummon then. Ooze ziss bird o' your Enry's, then? Rumour is 'e's elopin' with the family silver.

– Yer bloomin' fool. Yer doan know whatyer tawkin' about, yer muckspreader. This a shop or a farm?

She drew herself up and pushed the money across the counter.

– 'S all there. Yer needn't bother countin' it.

Dennis pushed his cap back and cleaned his ear with his best finger.

– Weren't me spreadin' the muck that day she come bouncin' 'er udders along The Colonnade...

– You moron. She's from a decent family with a darn sight more in her noddle than you ...

– Ohhhh yer know who I mean, then. Caught yer there, missus. I'm tellin' yer, gobble 'im up, she will. Gobble-gobble-gobble.

– Doan' be s' crude, you ape. I woan 'ave the likes o' you makin' disrespectful remarks 'bout my son's fiancey, jew'ear?

– Fiancey is she? Caw, 'e's gotta nerve, that boy o' yawn. Talk about fancy. Where's she gonna be 'angin 'er knickers out to dry then? In your back gardin?

– Won't be Awkhurst, fra start. My son's movin' up in the world, well away from the larks o' you.

– Oh yeah? What's she then, spacewoman? Boom-boom! She Thunderbird One then, or your Virgil 'ad his rocket up before?

– You filfy buffoon. 'Er father's prob'ly the County Sheriff for all you know.

– Whassat make Enry then? Deputy Dawg? Bang bang ...

– You'll laugh the other side o' your face one day, Dennis Balldock.

The bell rittled as she slammed the door. Dennis came out behind her singing *High Noon*:

Do not forsake me oh my darlinnnnnn'
Or miss our weddinggggggggg day-ayyyyyy.

I watched her make her way along The Colonnade. I heard the tobacco clap through my letterbox and she walked back unarmed. Dennis jumped out and shot her in the back with his lighter gun. When she'd gone I handed in the keys and hitched along that road I once took with Maxine, to Hardfarthing Hall. I didn't know exactly what I'd do there. Move in, hide like a stowaway in one of the wings, sneak down to the larder at night, or burn it to the ground with everyone in it.

twenty-six

Hardfarthing Hall was empty. They'd gone, fled me, left me
their empties. I knew about emptiness, about cubes of air with
doors and bare lightbulbs, the ringing in your ears and the smell
of dust up blackened nostrils. Where a click on your Bunny Club
lighter echoes like a shot gun, and your desert boots shuffle on the
floorboards like a plague of rats. Every door is a tea-chest lid prised
open with a gemmy. Every window you smash is an atomic bomb.
It was like breaking into a dream, like it hadn't happened that first
time round. That it only appeared if you held Maxine's hand. What
I'd found now was what appeared when you touched her wrists.
It was as if you're never present for the really important moments
of your own life. Like they're photographs you send away to be
developed, delaying the joy of being present at the real thing. That
way you avoid being who you are, I suppose. You're never an open
flower when the one drop of rain falls from the sky.

Then there are the things you already know, your ancestral
knowledge. You've already been there so you don't need to go
through it all again. I was thirteen when I broke into Oakfield, with
its pillared gates and a rhododendron jungle. The conker trees were
medieval and yielded canonballs, so this put it on our seasonal map.
Like all the old Hawkhurst mansions, it had something to make our
pockets or imaginations bulge. The fate of mansions was to stand
empty most of our childhood, waiting, till obliterated by creeper
and wisteria. Henry Winchester, Lord Mayor of London 1834/5,
built Oakfield. He entertained the Duke of Wellington there. In
1914 it became a military hospital and sheltered wounded Belgians.
According to experts, the house was only noted for its porch of fine
coupled Ionic columns. One of Old Waghorn's Bygone Books has
this photograph: chaps with pipes and officers' tunics lean against
the columns on their crutches. Others lounge at ease with bandaged
heads on canvas field chairs under the tall drawing room windows.
A nurse smiles because it's summer, and the men are safe. The war
memorials aren't built yet.

Even empty, Oakfield kept this atmosphere of lost summers and wounded soldiers passing through. Till it was driven away by the bulldozers, the councillors, the fat-fingered Tories. The Maxines, the room-at-the-toppers, selling off to the luxury hoteliers, the commuter homes, the wife-swappers. Our conker trees were felled, uprooted and burned. A road bulldozed through the grounds. Oakfield itself was left standing with a small back garden and a picket fence. By the pavement they built a big brick shed with a wooden cross. The varnished hardwood sign said Roman Catholic Church. There were hardly any Catholics in the village till then, just this houseful of grey-skirted Parker girls whose old man had left them for a barmaid or the bottle.

The split-level, double-garaged town-houses for the new catholics lapped the edges of the big house. We waited for its demolition. The windows rotted out, the wisteria was poisoned. Most of the rhododendrons were wrenched out by the hair. A wounded house stranded on an island of churned-up clay. Our interest in it declined. We weren't urbanogenic, and we weren't welcome down Oakfields. No Through Road, it said. Oakfield snobs mowing their fenceless lawns shouted at us: get back down your own way.

Then Sid Catt said there was a builder's sign outside Oakfield. They were doing it up for Lord Snooty.

So, after dark, in the dirty wet mist one February evening, me and Sid Catt sneaked round the back of Oakfield. It was me had to shin up the drainpipe and in through an open grill. I landed in the pantry toilet. A rusty key hanging on cobweb and string unclotted the back door lock after a few double twists. The wooden floorboard creaked under our shoes. I don't know what we expected. This was no cartoon. Sid Catt looked for cash, I went for the atmosphere. I wanted to feel how snobs possessed a place like this, which route your daily life had to follow in somewhere so huge. But the smell of new pine and paint displaced any insight into that limbo between dereliction and renovation.

There was not a bent farthing in cash. There was nothing we needed. All we found was the debris of Fryer & Sons the Builders and Chiesman, Plumber. Then Sid Catt kicked over a row of empty beer bottles. I trampled in his panic and a set of tools flew sideways. I collided with his flailing elbows, blundering into the unshuttered drawing room where a street lamp zapped us bullseye. Sid Catt's face was leper yellow and he gawked through the big windows. I'd discovered what I came for after all. Disappointment. I've felt it since, when seeing Maxine stripped of all poetic decoration. Underneath, her ordinariness was stifling. Her lack of originality embarrassing.

I burgled a poxy torch, ratchet screwdriver and a two-bob penknife with just the bottle opener left. It fell through the rip in my old school blazer into the lining. There was nothing else to detain us, just cold tea in a thermos cup on an upturned tea-chest. Runt-brain was angry and smashed a beer bottle in the fireplace. I threw cold tea over new plasterboards.

Inside Hardfarthing Hall I had to start again, see what I really knew before Maxine made me distrust it all. Then I could turn off that leaking tap for a start, the one which trickled with gathering force till it entered Hawkhurst on the Four Throws side as the tidal wave sweeping us all off-course. The one that killed the old man and was busy drowning Small Mercy and Wayne and all my schoolmates in Borstal. The one on which the Christians surfed and bathed, the one which Parson Potter filled his buckets from. I could see it was left on deliberately now. It bled on the whole of England, seeped in from everywhere. But what could I do alone? Turn one off and ten more were turned on full. No, I'd tried politics and lost the deposit. I didn't have the glamour, or the parents. I wasn't a party-goer.

I walked the empty staircases, as if somewhere there was a room all furnished for who I was, what I could be. The clothes in the wardrobe, the tools of the trade on the table. And you know, it even felt like Swattenden on a Saturday morning, that empty house, when you went in for football and it was just a deserted mansion, probably built by the same bloke. Stripped of its nine hundred cowering boys, it lost its authority. You could smash its windows and scratch *Ranyor is a cunt* on his door, but you didn't. It was like seeing a master on a Saturday, doing his shopping in his black A30, seedy old batchelor who'd bought himself a Mars Bar to eat in front of the telly, on his own. On his own till Monday morning. A stabbing of embarrassed pain went through you, and even in your ignorance you felt sorry for the wanker you called Puffing Billy, the bloke who only taught the C stream cories about artesian wells when he'd never even seen one himself. Yeah, whatever I did, whatever I became, I'd have to do it for the likes of Puffing Billy too, and even the old man, why not. It wasn't their fault the Maxines took it all and even burned their leftovers. Just so we wouldn't get our hands on whatever it was they thought they had.

I stayed on in Hardfarthing Hall for a month. It took me a month, once I'd recognised my way through this. I found the tins of paint in the sheds. You wouldn't believe how hard it was to write your first collection of poetry all over a flaming great mansion. There were thirty-four rooms, that's four pages a room. A volume of one hundred and thirty-six pages. I came up with the words at last, damned that stream into a reservoir. The poems rose in paint onto every wall in the house, the whole wall, poems ten feet high, all without a ladder, just precarious scaffoldings made of pantry shelves and tree branches, a tea-chest and a broken chair. I lived off rusty tins of grub from the now shelfless pantry, stale packets of soup they'd left behind. I went into the village twice to get tobacco, which is probably when suspicions were aroused. But I'd finished it before they came, Z Cars with dogs and loud hailers.

At Oakfield me and Sid Catt had been knabbed by Sgt Wyman. Once outside, Sid pranced about like he'd won the pools, immune to detection. I was tiptoeing along the mossy border. Sid was bragging in the gravel drive. Giant tape measure big as a discus. G-cramp, plumbline, light switch. Even the fuckin' salt pot for old Cheisman's boiled egg. There was a noise like an owl or nightjar. Blip-blip. My ornithology wasn't as sharp as Sid's. His was the lightening reflex of a born coward. He knock-kneed himself invisible as I was swiped across the guts by Sergeant Wyman's searchlight. Like a streak of shite I was in the bushes too, dumping my pocket linings right down to the fluff.

– COME ON, SONNY JIM, SHOW YERSELF.

I stepped into the beam, hearing a light switch and salt-pot clip through wet branches into leaf mould. Sergeant Wyman sat like a rhino on his bike.

– Now laddie, where's yer mate?

– What mate?

I wasn't shielding him from the law, the runt. I was just ashamed to be found with him and sure he'd blame me. Wyman cupped his hands into a megaphone.

– LISTEN, LADDIE. IF YOU DONT LEAVE THEM BUSHES

ON A COUNT OF TEN I'LL 'AVE YOUR GUTS F' GARTERS.
1 ... 2 ... 3 ...

At seven there was a rat scuffle in the bushes and Sid legged it across the gap towards the backyard thinking he could escape over the golf course. Wyman was off his noddy like a canonball.

– STAND STILL, LADDIE, OR I SHOOT.

Poor Sid, face like a plastic owl. Really believed he had a gun. Sergeant Wyman turned to me with a sorry expression.

– Ooz zat then, Scotch Mist?

Scotch Mist got a good swipe which had him booing. We got the dire warning treatment on account of our dads being 'good fellas.'

This time Z-Cars came with blazing sirens. And still I never betrayed her. They had me up against the car and the top pig gave me a karate chop to the kidneys. I said I hadn't knicked anything, that the place was empty, I'd simply turned it into a book for Maxine. I showed them her letter, the permission I had to be there, even:

Good luck, sweetheart; do not even despair over another: none of us are worth it. Perhaps later, when you feel less hateful towards me, we can write as friends. As always, I will wonder how you are getting on. I was so flattered that you would dedicate a book to me – perhaps one day, having written some melancholy poems of autumn, you still will? A leaf half-remembered, blown to the wind.

The title was 'Scotch Mist,' and this I'd painted along the outside wall, with broom handles and rollers, by leaning from the windows. It was fantastic. I was handcuffed and we went into the house. I said I was the poetry cracksman. We stood and read the title poem:

Scotch Mist – to Maxine.

You're on your own, your life's a blitz,
black-out blues on every window,
air raid sirens instead of ticking clocks.
Daylight is a seige for you.
Whether sudden or long drawn,
like putting profit back into the bank.
However much you make, it's bankruptcy and ruin all the
same.

The great accumulator. Index-linked.
Only one day, something's different.
You thought it was random and spiteful, the people it chooses.
Then afterwards you think: that's deliberate. I should've guessed.
You still don't know what it is, though, do you?
Is it clinical? Poetical? Criminal?
The 'clinical' is one step ahead of the environment.
The 'poetical' follows you round the world ever after.
The 'criminal' is scientifically immune.
Well, sweetheart, they're all ME.
They're all deja-vu. Sub judice. In camera. Out of tune. Doh-ray-me-fucked.

twenty-seven

S on of Dust might beat his knees at night and scream: I'm a sinner, Lord, forgive me: I took undue pride in my coffin lid today. But I'm not as duplicitous as him, even if, in his opinion, I need ego-trips like he needs his Fruit & Nut. So I threw those uncollected photos of my life away. I'd had that vision of myself, and I stuck to it. And here I am, oh yes, shimmied round them all, won that ego-trip of a lifetime, and I got the Fruit & Nut.

The Parson sent Son of Dust up to the County Asylum on the eve of my discharge. The magistrate had sent me there for three months' psychiatric evaluation. Three months scuffing over buffed lino like leaks from humanity's tap. Oiling your cogs with the three-in-one of cold piss, instant coffee and nicotine ghosts, sour side-up. Son of Dust came in a frock coat, carrying a black kind of Bible-cum-purse, great ideas for gifts in the Baptist Christmas Catalogue. His beard was trimmed square and he wore black cowboy boots.

– God Bless, he said, shaking my hand, diagram 4 in the Baptist First Aid handbook.

– Christ, man, I said, you won't get out of here looking like that. There's people like you in Wren ward. Been there thirty years.

– I've come straight from scripture conference, he said.

He was still gabbling in tongues. He just wasn't able to say to me: Parson Potter doesn't want you back in Hawkhurst.

– You know, I've been uh, turning my thoughts and prayers to your liddle problem, Hen. Yeah, I've even come up with some groovy ideas. I wanna help get you back on your feet. It breaks my heart, man, you're so talented. Luck's a bummer, yeah?

– No, bad luck's a bummer.

– Righdy, righdy. Err, Hen, friend, have you, like, mebbe ever thought of going to India, on the Magic Bus? I nearly went myself, man, you know that?

– No fuckin' money, I said.

– You can get there on fifty pounds. Liddle summer job, he said, two weeks picking strawberries and wow, gateway to experience.

Fifty pounds. He didn't even say quid anymore.

– Summer's over, I said, and anyway, do I want to pick strawberries with the Swattenden mums by day and listen to the ratbag squeeze all hope from the world by night?

– Listen, Hen, my friend, listen to me. This isn't, indeedy, you know, official like, but you know, the Parson's rilly got it together. The Hawkhurst Lighthouse, a social welfare fellowship, and eh, it's early days, yeah, but there might be some hardship funds going...

– Why does he go to all that effort? I said. Why don't I just open up a Barclays apartheid account and he can have God transfer the money. Or, better still, just have him beam the cash outside the back door.

– Ah, Hen, Hen, he's a good man, truly, he's godda soul that rilly shines. You broke his foot, you know. He lied for the first time in his life to save you. That was GBH, man.

– What did he say?

– He said the paperweight fell off the table. He missed Brim Stone's party, it was bad vibes, too gloomy.

– Well, you lied to get me there, so one lie deserves another. And do you know what he really said? He said: 'Fucking Jesus Christ Almighty.' Aren't we gonna find the poor-box missing a few quid after language like that? I mean, I don't offend anyone if I swear, but he's done GBH on God with that string of filth, the hypocrite.

– That's so, uh, cynical man. Real shameful.

– There's nothing more cynical than Baptist scripture. One day you'll all wake up and find the Parson's absconded with your sister, and the chapel float.

– That's a rilly filthy thought, Henry. She's engaged now, Delilah is. Anyway, Hen, I have to love you and leave you now, man. I've sown the good seed. Can I tell Parson Potter the good news?

– Spread the good news like margarine instead of butter. Tell him not to worry his little nylon socks off. I can be bought for two hundred pounds seraphim.

– God bless.

God's dead. I know this because he left me two hundred quid in his will, more than my old man left for his lifelong toil. That is, the will of God bequeathed me the funds due to some very fierce, constipation-busting prayer from the Parson. I'm a man of my word. I left Hawkhurst. I'll never see it again. I'll never break the

Parson's other foot or dance on my old man's grave. Or appear in the County Court for writing poetry on Maxine's walls. The joke's on them, the pure and the impure, the sinners and the saved. Maxine digging in her wrists for gold. Small Mercy weeping sleet while the sun shines. All the Baptists lamenting in their pit. Well, it's easy to sneer from afar when you're in paradise.

I can tell you how to get here, too. You get hold of Grace. She's from Lewisham, and sounds like all my cousins. Jesus, she stands in the car park outside the Accute Admissions Unit in the rain every day till you go out with her. Just gritting up your flares in the wet, slogging round the grounds, the patients' canteen, shoplifting down Maidstone.

One night there's a disco on Female Nines, a long stay ward, so you and Grace go over there and eat sausage rolls and take the piss out of the old hags with nurses making their arms go up and down to Beatles crap on an old Philips record player. Grace is weird. Not you-type weird, but scarey-jagged weird, and you want to dump her. After the disco you stand under the iron fire escape in the rain and light Number 10s. An hour to go before night medication. She won't stop talking, thousand words a minute, all about her weird-like feelings and that, so you're fungling her and smoking at the same time till you chuck the nub down and lever both her tits out as if you're playing snooker. But she's staring into the lamps and the rain as if you aren't there, yattin' and yattin' then singing some great new song she's just heard by 10 CC: *ah'm nod in la-arve, s'doan forgeddit, 's juss a silly phase ah'm goin' frew…*

You scub yourself against her as she sings till you come in your trousers.

– Less go back now, you say.

She hasn't noticed anything. It's early May, windy drizzle, blowing hot and cold, a foot in two seasons, the kind of day you caught your first chub on a fly down Bodiam, on the cane rod too and the old flyline your neighbour gave you. You remember it because you'd felt on the verge of something, a twelve-year-old achieving a thing incredibly sensible. This is the furthest off you can think of, the furthest off you want to be right then. A boy who knows who he is in a world where the horizon stops where it's supposed to stop. You'd even tied the fly yourself, and maybe if you'd heeded this opportunity you wouldn't've been wasting these moments in a mental hospital. There *will* be a vision of yourself. You know it's out there because, driving away from Hardfarthing Hall in a police car, you saw that young angry poet walking along a river bank. Just cling onto that and do your time.

Then, when they chuck you out, you go to Tunbridge Wells and get new heels put on your walking boots. You buy a train ticket from Shady Places Travel Agents, an old Boy Scout rucksack from the junk shops down Camden Road, spare cylinder for the camping gaz at Millets, new sketch book and German drawing pen from Goulden & Curry, *The Sign of Four* and *Nausea* from Halls second-hand bookshop. Go rugged, dump your Carnaby Street leftovers and your Kensington Market wings. Look instead like those pastoral Georgians with their tramping kits and gypsy kerchiefs. Me, I've kept the old man's red Tootal, goes inside the plaid shirt. You can decommission the bell-bottoms, too. They ring no more. The good Levi original, the Swiss Army knife.

On the train to Folkstone you read *The Sign of Four*, a kind of goodbye to old England. You drink coffee on the ferry at teatime and prepare your sketchbook with doodles of diminishing white cliffs. You turn round and face Dieppe, the Paris train is there, poised, curled on a bend, the harbour cranes, the adenoidal gulls, the long hotel accutely white and a smell that pinches. You're jubilant, you're in love again, and you are that poet. Only this time you're not here to resurrect the defunct beauty of others. You're here to scuff and rub that anger into a shine, the insults into freedom.

Ah, Dieppe. You think the evening sun's a wet scar in a gauze of cloud, and then you know, you bloody know that this time you've found your true epic. It will love and nurture you, it won't dump you for the sake of England, the petty affections, the plagiarisms of your detractors.

You stand on the quayside with the foot passengers, adjusting to what you really see. You hear the woodpecker chug of La Rosemarin as it brings in the lobsters. You don't read *Nausea* yet; there's too much to see, even if Dieppe was Sartre's Hawkhurst. There's a klaxon, a whistle, and on the train you stick your head out of the corridor windows with everybody else as you circle the town, high above the harbour with its booms and cranes swinging over a whitened sky. You descend once more into the streets, the harbour swings away to the left, the tips of cranes, flags on masts, gulls mobbing the lobster boat, and someone leans on a bicycle and waves at your train. You wave back, you wave back furiously and it's your first glimpse through the strange French windows, adjusting to what you see, a landscape rocking from the sway of train. A copper sky over fields that appear so much sooner than expected, fields like scattered pastel landscapes. They go on and on, all the way to Paris.

At dawn you strike out on foot from Tours, following the river Loire as far as the humped-back bridge at Savonnières. You don't need to hitch like you used to. Hawkhurst is not even a pin-drop in the silence here. Once every half-hour an old tin Citroen made of oil cans chugs by, some peasant like a glazed pot in a cap and a Gitane on his lip, a dog or a sack of spuds on the seat beside him. Not a commuting snob in sight. There's no shame in the decay here, no rush to fill the holes in the ground. The sunflowers light your way. Below the bridge, a mechanical excavator works the gravel. Fishermen stick like broken branches mid-stream and you lean on the wall and sketch them. In your rucksack, there's the six-piece smuggler's fishing rod you've made yourself, all packed into a leather tube a foot long, which maybe later, as the evening falls, you'll try on those greedy chub you can see supping on fat grey flies below the bridge.

For now, under the shade of the plane trees, you lay the feast on the wall: cheese, apples, bread, avocados, wine and crisps from a dusty VG store which smells of ripe Camembert and wine barrels. Nothing's prepared you for the real taste of these things. The swallows gather over the Loire, and you realise you've crossed it, this wild untameable river. You descend the worn steps and walk over the gravel shot with a hundred years of broken plates and pots and bones and smooth green glass. You couldn't cut your wrist with it if you tried. With your rag and your camping knife, you wash your hands, rinse out your tin mug. And you've made it, to that vision of yourself. You're a freedom fighter, a working class hero, a poet of nineteen years walking by the Loire.

Fiction from Two Ravens Press

The Long Delirious Burning Blue
Sharon Blackie

'I have been asleep for forty years. This is what I need: this fear, this risk, this wind rocking my wings. This is what I have been missing. This is what it means to be alive – up here, on the edge of death.'

Cat Munro's safe, carefully-controlled world as a corporate lawyer in Phoenix is disintegrating, and she is diagnosed with panic disorder just before her fortieth birthday. In a last-ditch attempt to regain control of her life, she faces up to her greatest fear of all: she decides to learn to fly. As she struggles to let go of old memories and the anxieties that have always held her back, Cat faces a choice: should she try to piece her old life back together again, or should she give in to the increasingly urgent compulsion to throw it all away?

Several thousand miles away in Scotland, Cat's mother Laura faces retirement and a growing sense of failure and futility. Alone for the first time in her life, she is forced to face the memories of her violent and abusive marriage, the alcoholism that followed, and her resulting fragile relationship with Cat. But then she joins the local storytelling circle. And as she becomes attuned to the mythical, watery landscape around her, she begins to reconstruct the story of her own life ...

From the excoriating heat of the Arizona desert to the misty flow of a north-west Highland sea-loch, Sharon Blackie's first novel presents us with landscape in all its transformative power. An honest and moving exploration of the complexities of mother-daughter relationships, *The Long Delirious Burning Blue* is above all a story of courage, endurance and redemption.

'An inspirational literary début; empathetic and mature. '
Margaret Graham

'Sharon Blackie writes with a real sense of truth and emotional depth about relationships between individuals, and between individuals and their environment. Her characters are figures in a landscape brought vividly, vibrantly to life.' *Nicholas Royle*

£8.99. ISBN 978-1-906120-17-7. Published February 2008.

Auschwitz
Angela Morgan Cutler

Auschwitz: a place where millions were killed and which thousands now visit each year. A mass grave – and a tourist destination. The focus of this work of autobiographical fiction is on the sightseers – the curious that are drawn to visit. It is a book that questions our need to look: what is there to uncover, other than the difficulty of peering into such a place and into a subject that has been obsessively documented, yet can never really be understood? How to write about Auschwitz in the twenty-first century, in a time when the last generation of survivors is soon to be lost?

This is also a book that searches for a personal story. It opens on a local bus that takes Angela, her husband En (whose mother survived the holocaust where most of her family did not) and their two sons to Auschwitz sixty years after the holocaust, and ends in a pine forest outside Minsk where En's grandparents were shot in May 1942.

The backbone of *Auschwitz* is a series of e-mails between the author and acclaimed Franco-American writer Raymond Federman. At the age of 14, Federman (now approaching 80) was hastily thrust into the small upstairs closet of their Paris apartment by his mother just before she, his father and two sisters were taken to Auschwitz, where they were killed. Federman also has spent a lifetime trying to find a language appropriate for the enormity of the holocaust and his part in its legacy, ultimately espousing laughterature – laughter as a means of survival.

This beautiful, powerful and innovative work experiments with new forms – correspondence, reflections, dreams, a travelogue – that mirror the fragmentary legacy of the holocaust itself and that, at the same time, capture its contradictions – and sometimes its absurdity.

'*Auschwitz* stands like a tombstone for our civilisation. Angela Morgan Cutler has brilliantly infiltrated the borders of this landscape of desolation. Somehow she has found a voice that reflects the enormity of the horrors perpetuated there without being stifled by them. Unsentimental and richly worked ... the words are more than mere messengers of thoughts and feelings---they glow with a life of their own ... the whole package quite inimitable: the rarest quality in literature.' *Henry Woolf*

£9.99. ISBN 978-1-906120-18-4. Published February 2008.

Love Letters from my Death-bed
Cynthia Rogerson

There's something very strange going on in Fairfax, California. Joe Johnson is on the hunt for dying people while his wife stares into space and flies land on her nose; the Snelling kids fester in a hippie backwater and pretend that they haven't just killed their grandfather; and Morag, multi-bigamist from the Scottish Highlands, makes some rash decisions when diagnosed with terminal cancer by Manuel – who may or may not be a doctor. Meanwhile, the ghost of Consuela threads her way through all the stories, oblivious to the ever-watching Connie – who sees everything from the attic of the Gentle Valleys Hospice.

Cynthia Rogerson's second novel is a funny and life-affirming tale about the courage to love in the face of death.

'Rogerson's prose has a wonderful energy and rhythm. She is a master storyteller whose love of language and black humour envelops the reader within the strange and strangely familiar, sometimes reminiscent of early John Irving. A delightfully funny and deeply touching book.'
Laura Hird, Scottish Review of Books

'Witty, wise and on occasions laugh-aloud funny. A tonic for all those concerned with living more fully while we can.' *Andrew Greig*

£8.99. ISBN 978-1-906120-00-9. Published April 2007.

Prince Rupert's Teardrop
Lisa Glass

Mary undresses and wades into the boating lake. She dives and opens her eyes. In the blur, she perceives the outline of a head – she reaches... A dead bird. But she will keep searching. Because Mary's mother, Meghranoush – a ninety-four year-old survivor of the genocide of Armenians by the Turkish army early in the twentieth century – has vanished. Mary is already known to the police: a serial telephoner, a reporter of wrongdoing, a nuisance. Her doctor talks of mental illness. But what has happened is not just inside her head. A trail of glass birds mocks her. A silver thimble shines at the riverbed – a thimble that belonged to her mother. A glassblower burns a body in a furnace and uses the ash to colour a vase. Rumours circulate of a monster stalking the women of Plymouth. Has her mother simply left – trying to escape the ghosts of genocide in her mind – or has she been abducted? It is left to this most unreliable and unpredictable of daughters to try to find her, in this moving, lyrical, and very powerful work.

'Lisa Glass writes with dazzling linguistic exuberance and a fearless imagination.' *R.N. Morris*

'A virtuoso stylist of the calibre of Rachel Cusk, Lisa Glass has created a powerful murder mystery, whose violent undercurrents flow from the bitter inheritance of the Armenian genocide.' *Stevie Davies*

'*Prince Rupert's Teardrop* digs into the macabre inside apparently mundane lives, and dissects it with relish, energy and compassion.'
Emma Darwin

£9.99. ISBN 978-1-906120-15-3. Published November 2007.

Parties
Tom Lappin

Gordon yearns for a little power; Richard wishes reality could match the romantic ideal of a perfect pop song; Grainne wants life to be a little more like Tolstoy. Beatrice looks on and tries to chronicle the disappointment of a generation measuring the years to the end of the twentieth century in parties.

Parties, the début novel by journalist Tom Lappin, is a scathing, insightful and profoundly human commentary on party politics and the corrupting effects of power. But above all it is a satire: a black comedy about young people getting older, and learning to be careful what they wish for, lest they end up finding it.

'Compelling and absorbing: the story of four friends growing up in the '80s and '90s, through the voyage from idealism to disillusion that was left-wing party politics through the turn of the century.'
Paul Torday (author of *Salmon Fishing in the Yemen*)

'... A fresh, funny, self-confident debut ...' *The Herald*

£9.99. ISBN 978-1-906120-11-5. Published October 2007

Nightingale
Peter Dorward

On 2nd August 1980 at 1pm, a bomb placed under a chair in the second class waiting room of the international railway station in Bologna exploded, resulting in the deaths of 85 people. Despite indictments and arrests, no convictions were ever secured. Exactly a year before the bombing, a young British couple disembark at the station and walk into town. He: pale blue eyes, white collarless shirt, baggy green army surplus trousers. She: twenty yards behind him. The woman he will marry, then eventually abandon. He is Don, she is Julia. Within 24 hours she'll leave for home – with the rest of their money – and he will wander into a bar called The Nightingale – and a labyrinthine world of extreme politics and terrorism. More than twenty years later their daughter Rosie, as naïve as her father was before her, will return to Bologna. Both Don – and his past – will follow...

'A gripping read ... moving, unsentimental, chilling and all-too-plausible ... The writing is vivid, economical and varied. It is alive to nuance and suggestion, dealing in emotional, cultural and psychological credibility.' *Andrew Greig, The Scotsman*

£9.99. ISBN 978-1-906120-09-2. Published September 2007.

For more information on these and other titles (novels, short fiction and poetry) and for extracts and author interviews, see our website.

Titles are available P&P-free direct from the publisher at
www.tworavenspress.com
or from any good bookshop.